"I don't know if anyone told you, but I'm adopting Ali," Sarah said.

A muscle twitched in Mike's jaw, as if he was unhappy about something, but when he spoke, his baritone was light and easy. "I'm glad for you, Sarah. You've wanted a child for a long time."

I wanted your child. She held back the words with all her might. Her spirit was reaching out, leaning toward him like he was her missing half, and why? The distance between them was so vast, the entire earth could fill it. Longing filled her, and she fought that, too. How had they grown so far apart?

* * *

Homecoming Heroes: Saving children and finding love deep in the heart of Texas.

JILLIAN HART

Jillian Hart grew up on her family's homestead where she raised cattle, rode horses and scribbled stories in her spare time. After earning her English degree from Whitman College, she worked in travel and advertising before selling her first novel. When Jillian isn't working on her next story, she can be found puttering in her rose garden, curled up with a good book and spending quiet evenings at home with her family.

Homefront Holiday
Jillian Hart

Steeple
Hill®

Published by Steeple Hill Books™

Special thanks and acknowledgment to
Jillian Hart for her contribution to
the Homecoming Heroes miniseries.

STEEPLE HILL BOOKS

Steeple
Hill®

Recycling programs
for this product may
not exist in your area.

ISBN-13: 978-0-373-87508-5
ISBN-10:   0-373-87508-8

HOMEFRONT HOLIDAY

www.SteepleHill.com

Printed in U.S.A.

Be kindly affectioned one to another with
brotherly love; in honor preferring one another.
—*Romans* 12:10

Chapter One

It was mid-December and the Coffee Break was busy, but not as busy as the street outside. Sarah Alpert drew her gaze away from the view through the wide glass window, where shoppers hurried about their seasonal tasks, to the little boy seated across the narrow table from her.

Ali. Her heart warmed simply from looking at him. She loved children, which was not surprising given she was a kindergarten teacher. But this one was special. She handed a paper napkin across the red plastic tabletop to her five-year-old foster son and student. "Hey, you have some hot chocolate on your chin."

He grinned, the charmer he was, showing his heart-tugging grin and the dimple in his left cheek. He scrubbed at the wrong spot on his chin.

Adoration filled her like Texas sunshine. She leaned forward, reaching over to rub at the right spot. Two swipes and the kid was clean. This sweetheart had proven to be the balm her wounded heart had needed. "Are you ready?"

Ali hopped down from his chair. "Yep. Can I call Dr. Mike yet?"

Mike. She tried not to flinch at that name.

"He hasn't called," Ali added. "He's comin' home, you know."

"Yes, I heard something like that."

"'Cuz I tol' you."

"About a thousand times." She managed to keep a smile on her face as she stood. "All right, sunshine, we have errands to do."

"Me and Dr. Mike are gonna get pizza and do lotsa stuff. We're buddies."

Sarah focused on her little boy and pretended he hadn't brought up Mike. Distraction, that was the key. "Which do you want to do first? Pick out our Christmas lights or mail our Christmas cards?"

"The lights!"

Her heart melted a little more. Already he was her family. She couldn't wait for the adoption to go through. Then he would be hers. Really and truly hers. "Coat on and zipped up. There's a cold wind out there."

"Yes, ma'am." Ali hopped down and his bright red sneakers—his favorite color—hit the floor with a squeak and a thump. His salute was the one Dr. Mike Montgomery had taught him. The two had met when Ali came in as a roadside-bomb casualty to Mike's MASH unit. The child had been injured, but his mother had been killed. Ali had formed a bond with Mike, and

Mike had helped arrange to send Ali to the States for lifesaving surgery.

Her heart twisted with an old pain. She and Mike had ended their engagement a year ago, but losing him would always hurt. She tucked that hurt away the best she could and put what she hoped was a big smile on her face.

"I get that." The little gentleman he was, Ali grabbed their garbage.

"Thank you." Sarah unhooked her jacket from the back of her chair and slipped into it, unable to take her eyes off the little boy as he trotted over to the receptacle near the door. He had to go up on tiptoe to dump it.

She hefted the shopping bags from beneath their table, slid her purse strap higher on her shoulder and held out her hand to her foster son. She was thankful every day that he was thriving, after all his losses. His grandfather Marlon, who had lived next door, had passed away last month. And while Ali had little time to get to know his grandfather, it was another loss all the same.

There were still shadows of his grief in his eyes that were always there, even when he smiled. Poor baby. She ran her fingertips through his fine, dark brown hair, hoping to comfort what could not be fixed.

"I get the door for you, Sarah." Ali trotted ahead of her, his sneakers thumping on the tile. He gave the door a mighty push.

"Thanks, kiddo. You are one strong boy." She complimented him as she sailed into the crisp overcast day and the busy sidewalk.

"I real strong now." Ali beamed with pride. His little

fingers wrapped around her hand, holding on so tight she could feel his need.

She held on tightly, too.

"Sarah, look!" Ali fastened his deep soulful eyes on a soldier in desert fatigues, who was walking down the sidewalk. The little boy turned on his heels to watch the infantryman stride away. "I'm gonna be a soldier *and* a doctor, just like Dr. Mike."

Her knees shook with every step she took. How long did it take a broken heart to mend? How long for regret to fade away? It took all her strength to swallow her sadness and hide every bit of her pain. "You couldn't pick a better man to be like."

"I know." Ali's confidence was simple and unshakable.

Hers was not so sturdy. Life had not been the same without Mike. She missed him more than she cared to admit. Still, she had done her best to make something of her life without him.

She knew Ali's next question would be about Dr. Mike, too. The boy was nothing if not persistent. Maybe it was best to try to distract him. "What color house lights should we buy?"

"Red." He thought a minute, tilting his head to one side. "No, wait. I want blue."

Sarah smiled. Ali lifted the sadness from her heart. Since this was his first American Christmas—and their first one together—she wanted to do it right. That's what she had to concentrate on: what mattered to her now.

"Dr. Mike!" Ali ripped his hand from hers and barreled down the sidewalk, darting between families

and a group of teenagers. He moved fast for a boy who'd just recovered from open-heart surgery! Sarah leaped after him, bags slapping against her knees as she caught up with him two steps before the busy intersection. She grabbed his hand, but Ali, the good, smart little boy he was, was already stopping on his own.

Before she could drag enough air past the panic clutching her throat and the stitch in her side to set him straight about running off like that, Ali jumped up and down, waving his free hand.

"Dr. Mike! There's Dr. Mike!"

Sarah squinted across the street through the traffic searching the pedestrians for him. For Mike. It took only one second for her gaze to find him. Perhaps she would always recognize his straight, strong back and wide, dependable shoulders, his short, dark blond hair and that confident, lanky stride.

Mike. Her pulse ground to a halt. All the ways she'd fallen out of love with him paled next to all the reasons she had fallen in love with him. He hadn't heard Ali's call above the rush of traffic as he stopped to look at a shop's window display. She could see his profile now; his handsome face was still the same with that square, honorable jaw and well-cut features.

What a relief it was to see him again. Her toes tingled with happiness, warring impossibly with her sadness. He was back safe, unharmed and whole.

Thank You, Lord. She sent the little prayer up with a piece of her heart. Just because Mike wasn't hers anymore didn't mean she couldn't pray for him. His happiness was more important than her own—even now. She had tried to talk herself out of her feelings, but they hadn't budged over the last year that he'd been away. Perhaps because of the way they had broken up right before he had gone off to war.

And now that she knew he was back home and unharmed, maybe she could let go of this sorrow. She planted her feet, hitched her purse back up on her shoulder and tightened her hold on Ali's hand. The light chose that moment to change to yellow and on to red. The traffic slowed and quieted, and Ali's "Dr. Mike!" must have reached the other side of the street because Mike looked up at the sound of his name. His eyes fastened to hers, just the way they used to do.

It was just nostalgia; that's what she told herself as she jerked her gaze from his. That's the only reason she could give to explain the startle in her heart that felt, impossibly, like joy at seeing him again.

I do not love him, she told herself. She wouldn't let herself again. She wished Mike well and that was all, nothing more. She would walk Ali right over to Mike and prove it to him.

And to herself.

Sarah. Mike stared in disbelief and then in dread as she started heading his way, with Ali's hand in hers. As she crossed the busy crosswalk, he had time to take her in. She looked different somehow. Her auburn hair was the same deep color and shone like silk in the afternoon sun. She was still as lovely as he'd remembered with her big blue eyes and soft, ready smile. She was wearing the wool coat she'd bought new around this time last year, right before they'd broken up. He couldn't quite put his finger on what exactly was different, but everything about her appeared a little brighter.

At the back of his mind came a small voice, one he didn't want to listen to. It was saying *She looks so good to you because you missed her so much.*

No, that was one voice he could not afford to listen to or encourage. He held his heart firm, dissolving away any lingering emotion. It was over and done with between him and Sarah. What he needed to focus on instead of their past was his little buddy—the boy he'd come to think of as a son.

It was a gift that Ali had come into his life. They'd had an instant connection in triage, when the nurse had called him over with worry in her eyes. Worry for a child caught in the middle of warfare. Ali had become his family over the last five months.

He thought of the paperwork he had on his truck seat, ready for his lawyer. Ali's adoption papers. He wanted the little boy with everything he had left. This last tour had taken out a big chunk of him, but that didn't matter now.

"Hello, Mike." Sarah's quiet, sweet voice could reach right in and grab hold of his heart if he let it.

"Hello, Sarah." He couldn't look at her. Time had not healed his wounds. He squared his shoulders, at a loss. Maybe he ought to just concentrate on Ali. The little dark-haired, dark-eyed boy was running toward him. True joy lit that little face.

"Dr. Mike! You came! You came!"

"Sure I did, buddy. Just like I promised. I didn't forget you." All the pain and exhaustion from this last year seemed to fade as the little boy flung out his arms and launched into the air. The world felt right as he caught the little fella in midair and swung him high before snuggling him to his chest.

Thin arms wrapped around Mike's neck so tight, it hurt. He set the boy on the ground. "Let me get a look at you. You're gettin' big."

"'Cuz I eat my veggies. But not broccoli." He shook his head. The two of them shared a great mutual dislike of that green vegetable.

"I told Sarah you come." Ali danced in place he was so happy. "You didn't call. I waited and waited. There was no ringing."

"Sorry about that." Mike swallowed, battling down the last of his emotions.

"I told him you were probably busy." Sarah spoke up in that quiet way of hers.

Her serene tone could lure him closer if he let it.

"I heard Whitney is back home and in the hospital." Sarah tried again to make conversation.

"You know Whitney Harpswell?" He spoke to her, but he kept staring at the crack in the sidewalk.

"Two girls in my class chose her and her husband for the Adopt a Soldier program, and we were writing to them before they disappeared." Sarah was genuinely concerned. "I heard that you found her."

"She was found by a villager woman. They brought

her to my MASH unit. I just recognized her." He resisted the need to look at Sarah and studied the boy instead. Ali's color was good. So was his energy level. His respiration clear and even. He'd heard reports through Dr. Nora Blake, the local surgeon handling Ali's case, and had talked to the boy as often as he could, but seeing was believing. There was nothing like being able to watch Ali hop eagerly in place to make the knot of worry relax in the center of his chest.

He wasn't a religious man, but he gave thanks right then and there standing in the middle of the street. He thanked God the boy had pulled through his risky surgery two months ago. He thought of all the others he'd treated—both soldier and civilian alike—who had not been so fortunate. Right from the start there had been something incredibly special about this plucky boy.

Ali stared up at Mike with his wide soulful eyes. "How come you didn't call? Why?"

Talk about feeling like a heel. Mike jammed his fists into his coat pockets and did his best to ignore Sarah standing protectively behind the boy. "I couldn't. I was on a plane flying home. I wanted to talk to you. You understand, right?"

"Okay. You gonna call me today?" Hope brightened the boy. "When?"

"I'm seeing you right now." Mike laughed as he scrubbed his hand over the kid's short brown hair. "Isn't that enough?"

"You gonna see me?" Hope lit the boy up like Christmas. "When?"

The kid wasn't understanding him. Mike shook his head, finding gentleness for the boy, though gentleness wasn't something he was good at. He felt awkward as he knelt down. He could feel the weight of Sarah's gaze and he ignored it. He focused on what mattered—this kid was going to be his son. "Sorry, buddy, this is it."

"But you said today." Ali cocked his head. His forehead scrunched up in thought. "You can come see me later. For supper? Sarah's gonna make my second favorite."

Macaroni and cheese, hot dogs and green beans. Mike didn't even have to ask. It had been his plan to stop by the commissary on the way to his duplex. Those foods were at the top of his shopping list. He didn't know how long it would take to get custody of the boy, but Mike liked being prepared. Now, if only he could keep ignoring the sensation of Sarah's gaze.

No such luck. He drew in a breath, gathered his courage and turned to face her. It took all his strength to keep the past from flashing through his mind, but it did anyway. Remembering that rainy October night as he'd stood huddled beneath her porch roof, wet with rain and ripped apart by her quiet words telling him it was over. Pain hit him, as fresh as a new wound.

Let it go, man. He squared his shoulders, met her gaze and held his heart cement-still. Let her see the man he was today. Resolute, unaffected and completely over her.

Was that a hint of panic flitting across her delicate features? He shifted his weight and stared down the sidewalk. Folks kept swerving around them, hurrying on with their lives. It felt surreal to stand here on a safe,

Texas street when a few days ago he had been surrounded by helicopters and artillery fire.

He started walking back a step. Unaffected, that's what he was. As cold as stone. "Don't worry, Sarah. I'll explain it to him."

"No, uh, Mike, I'm just—" She looked a little helpless, as if she were having a hard time wrestling with all of this. Her hand went to Ali's shoulder, a protective, motherly gesture, and he had never seen her eyes so sad.

He had to fight the natural urge to make it easier for her. He stormed over to the hardware store's glass door and yanked it open. All he'd ever wanted to do was to make things easier for her, but it was no longer his duty. This was the woman who hadn't wanted him. "Forget it, Sarah. You don't owe me any explanations. Ali, I promise I'll call you tonight, buddy."

"No, you're comin' to eat mac 'n' cheese, remember?"

Mike let the door swing closed. As much as he had to walk away from Sarah, he had to set things right with the kid. He owed that to the boy. He ran his hand over Ali's dark brown hair and ruffled it. "I can't make it tonight, buddy."

"You can't?" Some of the sparkle slid from the boy's midnight dark eyes. "How come?"

Mike gulped, seeing the disappointment set in. "I'm sorry."

"Okay." The boy's shoulders slumped. "Can you come tomorrow?"

"Tomorrow?" Mike crooked one eyebrow in surprise. How could he make the boy understand? He knelt down so he was eye level with the kid. But where did his gaze go?

To Sarah, standing on the busy sidewalk, next to the hardware store's front window displaying Christmas paraphernalia, keeping just enough distance to make it clear she wanted nothing to do with him.

"Dr. Mike?" Ali tugged on Mike's coat sleeve. "You don't like mac 'n' cheese?"

Mike gulped. He was capable of long, unrelenting shifts in the E.R., he didn't bat an eyelash when mortar rounds vibrated through the floor in his operating room, but having to see the hurt etched on the boy's face made his knees weak.

"I think there is only one solution and you're not going to like it." Sarah shook her head slowly, looking beautiful with the wind in her soft auburn hair and sadness vibrant in her jeweled blue eyes.

Remember, she means nothing to you. He glanced at his to-do list as if that were much more important than she had ever been to him. "I can't come to supper. I just got back."

"Today?"

"Midmorning."

"You probably have a lot to do to get settled."

"I do." His answer was clipped; as if he thought she was dismissing him.

"You probably have to run errands. Buy groceries."

"Right." He jammed both hands into his coat pockets.

There was no avoiding the truth that Mike was back,

that they would be running into him inevitably from time to time, for Prairie Springs was a small town. Ali would never stop adoring his hero, the man who had saved his life when he had been all alone.

It was hard for her, too. Every time she looked at this man, she saw that hero, too. She also saw the man she had once given everything in her heart to—and it hadn't been enough. It was hard to breathe past the ache that put in her throat.

The past is over, Sarah. You have to accept it. She took Ali by the hand. She had to be practical now. She had to accept that he adored Mike. Denying the doctor who had been his rock would only hurt Ali. That was not something she would do. But the alternative—the solution—was going to be hard for her. Terribly hard.

She eyed the doctor standing before her as objectively as possible. Travel fatigue lined his strong, handsome face and bruised the skin beneath his eyes.

Just say it, Sarah. She took a breath, gathered her courage and prayed that she sounded composed. Indifferent. Over him. "You may as well come for dinner tonight—"

"Yaaaaay!" Ali whooped, already looking just like any other American kid with his fist in the air and happiness on his face.

"Hold on there. I haven't answered yet." Mike chuckled in that warm, low rumble she had once loved so well. He was careful not to look directly at her. "Are you sure, Sarah?"

"It's for Ali's sake. We both understand that." Ali

may be jubilant, but Sarah felt the thunk of dread. She had been trying to prepare herself for this and there was still no way around it. Seeing how Mike was careful to keep distance between them, to be polite to her and reserved, made her think of all that had changed between them.

Handle this as you would any other guest coming to supper, Sarah thought. If Mike wasn't Mike but anyone else, what would she be saying right now? How would she be acting? Warmly, that's how. Friendly. She managed a small smile that she hoped was both. "We usually eat around five. Is that too early for you?"

"Nope. I'll be there." He gave her a curt nod.

Nothing personal in that nod. They would look like strangers standing on the street to anyone passing by. Strangers. The way it had to be, apparently. Nothing could make her sadder.

Mike smiled at Ali in that genuine, amazing way that made his hazel eyes golden. "I'll see you when the big hand's on twelve and the little hand's on five. Deal?"

"Deal." Ali's grin couldn't be any wider.

"You be good for Sarah until then, ya hear?" His voice dipped kindly, rumbling deep in his chest.

Sarah held her heart very, very still.

Ali held up one hand to wave. "Bye, Dr. Mike. See you later alligator."

"I'll see y'all later," he called over his shoulder, striding away fast.

Sarah didn't know why that struck her. Mike had been so far away for so long that distance between them was nothing new. It had happened well before he had decided to tear their love apart.

Of course, it had all been her fault. Hers. She had laid down the ultimatum for him to marry her or reenlist. She had known how committed he was to serving his country. Hadn't she known down deep that Mike had never loved her that much?

The proof of it was walking away, taking a part of her with him.

No amount of determination, dignity or willpower could change the truth—the truth she was just now seeing. She wasn't over Mike Montgomery after all. Not a little bit, not even close.

"Sarah?" Ali's hand caught hers and held on so tight. "Dr. Mike is great. I love him."

She tore her gaze away from the man, still visible among the sidewalk full of holiday shoppers. She turned her back and she still felt that awful longing.

Sarah drew in a shaky breath. "Let's go."

Chapter Two

He was just doing the right thing, Mike told himself as he pocketed the change in the hustle and bustle of the busy florist's. It wasn't as if he could show up without a hostess gift, right?

Across the small counter, Mrs. Neville, who had been a friend of his mom's back in the day, shut the cash register drawer and offered him a smile along with the bouquet of daisies trimmed and wrapped in festive paper.

"Are these for a young lady?" Mrs. Neville handed over the flowers with her question. "Next time I would recommend roses."

"It's not what you think." He took the flowers. He had avoided the roses on purpose. He didn't want Sarah to get the wrong idea—he had moved on. "I've been invited to dinner. Not the romantic kind."

"What a shame. A doctor like you," Mrs. Neville said with a tsk. "I can't believe a nice woman hasn't snapped you right up."

"Maybe I'd rather not be snapped."

"Oh, you young men. You'll want to settle down one day. You know, your mama, rest her soul, would be so proud of you."

"Thank you, ma'am. You have a good day." He gave her a quick salute and left the store.

He couldn't help thinking about his mom, who had been gone a long time. Cancer had taken her not long after his dad was killed in action. Mike had always thought that she died of a broken heart, for she had loved his dad too much. That had been a tough time in his life. He had been finishing his bachelors in chemistry, already of legal age and on his own. Sarah had been there for him. He wondered what his mama would think of what he'd made of his life. Would she understand what had happened with Sarah?

He was halfway to her house when his foot kept easing up on the gas pedal. It wasn't hard to figure out the reason why: Sarah. The past weighed like ballast. Over the last year he'd been busy enough with an all-consuming job, hoping to forget her.

So, why hadn't he? Time had helped, but not completely. When thoughts of her surfaced, it was like being battered by hurricane winds at sea. It was hard to keep bitterness from taking him down. He'd loved her with all he had to give, and it hadn't been enough.

Well, he hoped she found what she wanted.

Her little yellow house on the tree-lined street looked changed, too. A bicycle with training wheels was parked on the front lawn. A ladder was pushed up against the outside wall of the garage. The wicker love seat on the small porch held Clarence the cat. He sat on alert, watching through slitted eyes as Mike pulled into the driveway.

Well, some things did stay the same, Mike thought, as he cut the engine and climbed out of his truck. Clarence, apparently remembering him, laid his ears flat against his head.

Fortunately, the screen door chose that moment to slam open and there was Ali pounding down the steps. "Dr. Mike! Dr. Mike! I got every color ones!"

"That's good, buddy." Mike pocketed his keys. "Every color what?"

"Lights. For the roof."

Sarah stepped out onto the porch and ran a comforting hand over her cat's orange head. She said nothing, but the breeze swung the curled ends of her hair and the sunlight framed her with gold.

Don't feel a thing, man. He squared his shoulders and managed to take what he hoped looked like a solid, confident step toward the little boy.

"I gotta pick 'em out. I got all the colors." Ali's fists pumped as he ran down the walkway. "They flash like police lights."

"Lucky me." Sarah gave a wry grin.

The sound of her voice, sweet and low, still got to him. Mike swallowed hard. Coming over had been a mistake. He nodded toward the garage wall. "Is that the reason for the ladder? You're going to put up Christmas lights?"

"Guilty."

"I've never known you to climb a ladder."

"I have had to learn to do a few new things since I've been on my own."

Her quiet answer surprised him; she seemed calm and steady, centered, although she was watching him with the saddest eyes.

He had to try again.

Careful now, he thought. He took the daisies and the shopping bag he'd brought with him and shut the truck door. "Maybe I'd best stick around and climb that ladder for you."

"Oh, no, I didn't mean—" She held up one hand, which had been petting the cat, and the cat glared at him again.

"Dr. Mike?" Ali's gaze was glued to the gift bag and the flowers. "Who is those for?"

"The bag is for you."

Yet as dear as the boy was to him, it was the woman standing in the background that seemed to draw Mike's gaze and to keep it. The blue cable-knit sweater she wore complemented her creamy complexion and the soft red of her hair, making her look like a summer rose out of season.

The unveiled look of love on her face as she gazed at the small boy made him feel humbled and somehow ashamed. He loved Ali, but now he realized he hadn't considered that Sarah, as his foster mother, would have to give him up if he adopted him.

"Wow!" Ali's excitement carried over the sound of rumpling shopping bag. "A soccer ball!"

"Can you give these to Sarah?" He fought to say her name without inflection. He made sure his voice carried to where she stood on the porch. "A gift for the cook."

He wanted it to be clear.

"Okay!" The boy's happiness was contagious as he hurried to do as he'd been asked. He grabbed the daisies in both hands and ran the small bouquet to Sarah.

"Thank you, Ali. Mike, thank you, too." Judging by the unaffected tone of her voice, she was at peace over their breakup.

He was, too. He turned his back, so he wouldn't see her walking away with his flowers in her arms.

Daisies. Sarah tossed the paper they had come in into the kitchen garbage can. Mike was thoughtful; she had to give him that. She never thought she would be looking over the counter to see him standing in her living room, a pure soldier out of place against her chintz and gingham decor. How could she ever have thought she could get over that man?

Because telling herself she could had gotten her through life without him.

"Dr. Mike, I can kick good."

"That doesn't surprise me one bit." Mike ruffled Ali's hair. "If it's all right with Sarah, why don't you take me out in the backyard and show me?"

"Can I, Sarah?"

She looked into the pleading, delighted eyes of her foster son and couldn't say no. "You've got time before dinner is on the—"

Sneakers beat against the hardwood floors and the French door in the living room was wrenched open.

"—table," she finished.

"It's good to see him so active." Mike took a more leisurely pace, his presence filling the small room. "The first time I saw him in triage, hurting and little and scared—" He fell silent, keeping his emotions to himself.

Sarah's knees weakened at the picture that created in her mind—a picture she squeezed out as soon as it lodged there. It was too much to imagine Ali like that. What she *could* see was Mike watching over the boy, one hundred percent committed to saving him. Maybe that was the message God had been trying to get into her head.

She set the vase on the counter. "It must be rewarding for you to see him happy and playing."

"He's more than that. He's thriving, Sarah. After all he's been through—" Mike swallowed hard and looked away, clearly emotional.

Or as emotional as she had ever seen him. "You had a hand in his recovery."

"I didn't do much."

"You performed the emergency surgery that patched him up and got him here. Dr. Blake told me what a fine job you did." So many emotions were swirling around inside her that she couldn't begin to separate them. She stepped around the edge of the counter, wanting to be closer to him. "I don't know if anyone has told you, but I'm adopting Ali. I've fallen in love with him. I couldn't help it."

A muscle ticked in his jaw as if he was unhappy about something, and when he spoke his baritone was strained and raw. "You're adopting him?"

"I filed the papers last week."

"Last week?"

"You look surprised. I'm sorry if you don't approve, Mike—"

"No, it's not that." He couldn't seem to make his thoughts move past her words. His usually clear, crisp, problem-solving mind had broken down. He shook his head, but it didn't help.

"I just love him so much." Sarah, so sweet and bright and beautiful, turned on the water at the sink. She pumped soap into her small, slender hands. The fall of the overhead light seemed to spotlight her, drawing his gaze and his heart, forcing him to remember how dear to him she had always been.

His ripped-out heart hurt beyond bearing. It wasn't fair. It wasn't right. He shouldn't have to look at her like this, being tied up in knots. He didn't love her, not anymore. But it surprised him that his memories of her were still alive and dear. Memories of the quiet evenings they had spent together in this kitchen fixing meals, laughing over nothing, their conversations easy.

Maybe what hurt was that she had never loved him enough, the way he had always loved her. Her affection for the boy was plain to see. It transformed her. She was glowing.

He yanked open the French door and the agony hit. Ali was not going to be his. Bleakness battered him like a desert windstorm. He tried to tell himself that he'd lost nothing, at least not anything that hadn't been his at the start.

The trouble was, it didn't feel that way. He wrestled down the last of his feelings. He caught a glimpse of Sarah as he closed the door. Sarah's big blue eyes filled with regret and sadness. Pain clutched in his chest. She could still get to him.

The sinking sun hit him square in the eye as he crossed the little stone patio.

"Dr. Mike! Look! I'm the best kicker." Ali dropped the soccer ball and gave it a boot with his sneakers.

Who was he kidding? He had lost everything. He had lost his chance for this child. It was another hard blow in a year full of them.

"That's the best kick I've ever seen," he told Ali, and ran to retrieve the ball.

What had come over Mike? Sarah's heart felt heavy as she pulled the steamer package from the microwave. She had asked him over to dinner for Ali's sake, definitely not for hers. She tore open the package and poured the piping hot green beans into a serving bowl. She wanted to be over him. She prayed to be over him. So why wasn't she?

She dropped a spoon into the bowl and carried it to the table. Maybe the reason why wasn't such a mystery. Outside in the thinning daylight Ali kicked the ball to Mike, who gave a gentle return kick, sending Ali running and laughing. The faint sound of it warmed the air with joy.

It was like something out of her lost dreams to see Mike playing with a little boy in this backyard. How many times had she pictured that over the years she had been waiting for him to commit? She set the bowl on the table, filled with remorse. She had meant to push him closer to her, when all she did was push him away. She had let go of her dreams when she watched him board the transport plane that had carried him off to war.

Now, those dreams taunted her once again with what she could never have.

Don't think about it, she told herself as she crossed to the French door. Ali had kicked the ball again and Mike pretended to miss, making the little boy clap his hands and laugh with glee. Her feet came to a stop and she stood there watching the man with her broken heart on her sleeve. Mike would be a great dad one day. She had always known that. His concern for children was one of the first things she had loved about him.

You weren't going to think about that, remember? She shook herself, gathered her fortitude and opened the door. "Dinner is ready."

"Aw, just one more kick," Ali pleaded.

As if she could easily say no to that sweet face. She knew Mike was watching her; she could feel the burn of his gaze.

"One more, kiddo, then in you come," she called out. "I have mac 'n' cheese waiting."

"Yay!" Ali dropped the ball, gave it a kick and sent it reeling into the fence.

Mike's low rumbling voice as he commented on that

professional-style kick stuck with her as she retreated into the safety of her little house. Why did she feel choked up? She went to the sink, set out an extra hand towel for the two of them and fetched milk from the fridge.

Mike and Ali burst into the living room. The crisp evening air blew in with them, and their happiness warmed the place like fire in a hearth.

"Something smells good," Mike complimented as he shut the door behind them.

"Yum." Ali raced through the house, his sneakers thudding on the wood floor, beaming with excitement. "We put up the lights after, right?"

"As soon as your plate is clean."

"Yippee." Ali went up on tiptoe at the kitchen sink. It was their evening thing for Sarah to scoop him up so he could reach the faucet to wash his hands.

But Mike was there, chuckling deep in his throat. "Let me help you, little buddy."

"I can almost reach," Ali insisted, although he had a long way to go.

"I can't believe how big you've gotten." Mike grabbed the boy around the middle and hefted him up.

Ali laughed, a blessed sound. Sarah tore her gaze away from the man and child, so natural with one another. She set the milk carton on the edge of the table. Her hand was too shaky to pour. Memories she had tucked away came back to her—of Mike's deep baritone rumbling in her kitchen, talking of his work and of his dreams, captivating her then just as surely as she was now.

The distance between them now was so vast, the entire earth could fit in it. He was no longer hers to love. She had blown any chance with him. He stood military straight, with tension hard in the line of his jaw. His shoulders were rigid. His rugged face tight with tension. She still knew him so well, she could read how unhappy he was to be here. How unhappy he was to be near *her.*

She filled three glasses with milk, holding her feelings still as the man and boy toweled off and tromped her way.

"I see Clarence is still ruling the roost." Mike took the chair across the table from her—his chair.

She swallowed hard, determined to stay in the present. The trouble was, the man who sat across from her looked changed, too. The year had been a hard one. He didn't need to say a word for her to know. Sympathy wrapped around her heart, taking it over. What happened to him? She waited for Ali to climb into his chair, the cutie. Mike wasn't the only one who had changed. The little boy looked ten times happier with his hero at the table.

Life had a way of changing everyone, she realized. The last year had been hard for all three of them. Ali had lost his family and survived heart surgery. Mike had the Army and all that he had seen in a war zone. And she had learned how to live without the man she loved. Without a major piece of her soul.

"We say grace, Mike," she said gently as he reached for his glass of milk.

"Grace?" Surprise momentarily chased away the hardness on his face. "You say grace now?"

"I'm a Christian now." She wondered if he remembered the few times they had attended Sunday services at the church in town.

"That's a change." His tone was neutral and his face as unreadable as stone.

"A lot of things have changed since you've been gone." She wished she could be the strong, unaffected woman she wanted to be. But the truth was, she would always be vulnerable and moved by Dr. Mike Montgomery.

She bowed her head, folded her hands, and said the blessing.

"What do you think, buddy?" On top of the ladder perched against Sarah's roofline, Mike waited patiently for the boy down below to appraise his handiwork.

Ali's face scrunched up as he thought. "I like the red ones."

Mike considered the gigantic red bulbs that glowed like Rudolph's nose in the gathering twilight—or about fifty Rudolph's noses. "Do you want me to put the multicolored strings up on the porch?"

"No. I want 'em here." Ali padded over to point up at the roofline. "I want 'em *both*."

"Up here, together?"

"Yep."

Mike noticed Clarence was still on his cushion. The cat's ears had gone back as if he understood the conversation perfectly. "Any chance I can change your mind?"

"No." Ali's charming grin clinched it.

"Fine. You're the boss." Mike grinned back. "I'm comin' down for them."

He had no sooner touched his boots to the ground when Ali, bouncing in place, held up a handful of the smaller twinkle lights. The kid radiated so much joy that his feet were leaving the ground. Mike was glad he'd decided to come. He loved the boy like a son. What was that, compared with his own awkwardness around Sarah? He was a soldier; he could handle it.

"These are blinkers," Ali explained. "Sarah said that was special."

Mike chuckled, fighting the instinct to glance to the house where the front windows might afford him a view of her. It was habit, nothing more. He took the string of lights Ali offered. He could picture Sarah standing in the store saying "that was special," with a roll of her eyes, putting a bright face on everything, even her personal dislike of flashing things.

After he unplugged the extension cord, he tested the ladder just to be sure before climbing back on it. Sarah might not like blinkers, but he wasn't overly fond of heights.

He had to keep his gaze down, on the porch, as he made his way back to the top of the ladder, fighting to keep from looking for her through the windows. Clarence grimaced at Mike and gave him a disgruntled hiss.

"I'm not steppin' on his tail." Ali tipped his head back to explain seriously.

"I see that." Mike braced his body against the roof and plugged the new string into the outlet of the red.

"I did that once when I first come." Ali had kept up a steady stream of talk all the while the first layer of lights had gone up. Looked like he was about to do the same the whole evening through.

Mike grinned. "I bet Clarence didn't like that."

"Nope. He didn't get hurt, but I didn't mean it." Ali gulped. "So's I look down now. So I don't trip on him."

"That's mighty thoughtful of you."

"Yeah." Ali sighed, as if pleased with himself.

. Mike felt his grin stretch wider across his face. His chest hitched a notch, but Ali's place was with Sarah. And if there was one place that Mike didn't belong, it was here. How was he going to explain that to the kid?

He was at a loss. He hooked the coated wire through the plastic hook he'd inserted earlier beneath the edge of shingles and went onto the next. He didn't want to think about a future without Ali. It was as bleak as the one without Sarah. Sadness flattened him.

No emotions allowed, Montgomery. Remember? Mike hooked in the next length of wire, stretched it out. He peered down through the space between his feet to the little supervisor down below. "How does it look, boss? Okay?"

"Okay." Ali gave him a thumbs-up. "They gonna blink, right?"

"When I plug 'em in they will."

"I can't wait." Ali danced in place, unable to keep still, getting close to Clarence, whose ears returned to their normal position. The cat lifted his head expectantly.

How about that? Mike mused as he descended the

ladder to move it over a few feet. The prickly feline liked five-year-old boys. Through all the years he had dated Sarah, he had always thought Clarence was opposed to all human males in general. Apparently it was just him.

Yep, he thought as his boots hit the ground and the cat's ears went back. It's just me.

The good news for Clarence was that after tonight, he would never need to be disgruntled over Mike visiting again. He hiked the ladder over and started back up. "Are you and Clarence good buddies?"

"He loves me." Ali gave the fuzzy cat a gentle squeeze.

Clarence squinted his eyes, tolerating the affection. Mike shook his head, grasping the next ladder rung, and his gaze fell on the front window. This was a different angle, and there was Sarah setting a serving tray on the coffee table. He caught a glimpse of decorated chocolate cupcakes on plastic cartoon plates, bright yellow paper napkins and a small dish of Christmas-colored candies, and Sarah.

She was still as enchanting as ever with her floral-patterned furniture and ruffles everywhere, of her favorite books—children's books, of course—on the built-in bookcase next to the fireplace, nearby so she could read them anytime. She moved to the fireplace and hit a light switch. Gas flames curled over logs, the soft light haloing her like the dream she used to be for him.

She was a hard habit to break. He'd thought he had accomplished that. That had been the best thing about his deployment—he didn't have time to think about her and dwell on what he'd lost. He'd gotten over her.

Or so he'd thought. But not enough, apparently. He pried his gaze away and carefully worked the kink out of the light string. Now he could see there was still debris left from the breakup. Debris he had to clean out like shrapnel from an open wound. With each cut of his scalpel, he had to remove every last bit. It was that simple. Sad, true, but it had to be done. There was no other way.

Chapter Three

"Can they blink now?" Ali was craning his neck, trying to see as much as he could from the driveway. Mike had finished putting up the second string of lights at the far end of the house.

"Wait till I come down, ya hear?"

"Yes, sir."

As he climbed down, Mike listened to the thump, thump of Ali's sneakers on the cement as he bounced up and down, unable to hold back his excitement.

Ali caught his hand and tugged. "C'mon. Hurry!"

Mike's lungs seized up. The images of what he had let himself think about back in the desert took him over—images of what it would be like to have Ali for his son. Cooking dinner, taking him to school, taping crayon masterpieces to the refrigerator, hanging Christmas lights from the roof.

Not possible now, Mike thought as he knelt down at

the gutter spout. Looks like he would have to carve those feelings out, too.

One end of the orange extension cord snaked up behind the downspout, and the other half was on the ground, just as he'd left it. He handed the plug to Ali. "You do the honors."

"Can I? Oh, boy!" Ali's eyes widened and grasped it fast. He wasted no time getting the short distance to the outside outlet. Mike knelt down beside him to hold back the outlet's cover and helped him position the plug. It connected, colored light flared like fireworks against the dark sky and Ali clapped. "Looky. It's blinkin'."

"Good job, soldier."

Ali straightened up and lifted his hand to his brow to salute. "I'm gonna be just like you."

His throat closed and he stared at the flashing lights adorning Sarah's little house until they no longer blurred. But now, he realized what he had lost. This little boy. He would never have him for a son.

"I love it. I love it." Ali clasped his hands together, transfixed. "I love it! I want more. Can we do more, Dr. Mike? *Pleeeease?*"

"You want *more?*" He hoped his voice sounded normal. "Isn't this enough?"

"No, sir." Eyes wide, face happy, dancing in place, Ali was obviously thriving here with Sarah.

Could he fight for the right to adopt Ali? Should he? Maybe that was the bigger question. Ali had lost everyone he had loved; he did not need to lose Sarah, too.

Mike shoved his hands in his pockets and rocked

back on his heels. *Turn off your heart, man. Just turn it off.* He didn't let his gaze stray to the golden light of the window, where he might see Sarah. "You need enough lights for the Christmas tree, don't you?"

"But I want lots." Ali jumped in place. "So they flash and flash."

A chuckle broke loose. "If I were you, I would beg Sarah to put the Christmas tree right at that big window there, so you can see the lights from the front of the house, too."

"Yeah. Cool." Ali clasped his hands together. "Those lights flash. That's what Sarah said."

It amazed him how fast the boy was acclimating to his new country and new life with Sarah. Sure, being in school now with kids his own age helped, but it also said a lot about Ali's resilience and Sarah's love for him. Mike wrestled down his bitterness.

"Sarah!" Ali bounded away, full of energy and pounded up the porch steps. "Sarah!"

"Who's making all this noise out here?" Sarah's gentle voice was full of laughter. "I can't believe it's you, Ali. For a minute there, I thought it was Clarence."

Ali laughed and it was a precious sound, full of glee. "No, it's me! You gotta come see."

Mike had forgotten Sarah's charm. Maybe because it tore him apart to remember. But there it was, in the sweeping smile and brilliant eyes as she scooped her cat into her arms like a furry baby. She lugged him with her as she padded down the steps, washed in the jeweled glow from the lights. He could hear the cat's rusty purr as Sarah breezed near.

"You boys did a great job," she praised. "Ali, do those lights blink enough for you?"

"No! I want more."

"Those are the flashiest lights we could find in the store, silly boy." Warm gentle love, that was Sarah's voice. It was no surprise why Ali's gaze was one hundred percent pure adoration. Even when she was upset, which she had to be having him here, she was kind. "Mike, thanks for helping out. I never could have done such a good job."

"No problem." His voice sounded choked as the air pressure changed and the steel walls around his heart buckled. The several feet separating them seemed to vanish as they gazed up at the lights together, as if shoulder to shoulder.

You don't feel a thing, Montgomery, he ordered himself. *You will not feel one single thing.*

"Do you boys want to come in and warm up?" Her voice moved through him like a melody. "I've got chocolate cupcakes and cocoa for you."

"Oh, boy. I do!" Ali clapped his hands. "That's my favorite."

"Yes, I know, cutie. It used to be Mike's favorite, too." Her gaze pinned him with a quiet question. In the silence settling between them she was asking him to stay.

"Dr. Mike." Ali grabbed his hand and tugged. "We're alike."

Emotion lodged in his throat, burned behind his eyes. He wanted to stay for the boy's sake, but how would this end? Ali would soon belong to Sarah legally, and there was no future for Mike here. He thought of the span of life he had traveled without her. He had covered too much ground to go back. He had too much pride to keep looking the woman, who had ripped him to pieces, in the face.

He took a backward step. "I sure would like to stay with you, Ali, but I gotta get back."

"I don't want you to go."

Looking into those honest eyes made the lump in his throat harder to swallow. He missed the boy. Months ago when he had sent the boy off for his flight to the States, the desert outpost had been lonely without him.

All gone now. He squared his shoulders and put away those memories, those feelings. "I have to go. I'll give you a call tomorrow. How's that?"

"When tomorrow?" Ali's grip grew tight enough to cut off circulation. "What time are you gonna call?"

He saw pain for the boy soft on Sarah's beautiful face, but he did what he had to do. The boy wasn't his to love. The woman never really had been. He did an about-face and plucked his truck keys from his pocket. Tomorrow was Sunday. "How about lunchtime? Before noon."

"But I wanna see you, Dr. Mike." Ali's happiness dimmed, and the grief that his smile had been covering up was heartbreaking. "I waited and waited. Just like you said. We are gonna get pizza right away. You promised."

"I did." Pressure built behind his solar plexus. It wasn't just guilt. It wasn't just disappointment. How much had Ali been counting on getting together? Mike thought of all their phone conversations, and all the veiled suggestions he had made to do things with him. At the time, he had been feeling out the idea of adoption and picturing himself in the role as dad. Now he saw that Ali may have heard them as promises.

He winced. The last thing he wanted to do was to hurt the boy. How on earth was he going to be able to fix this? If he saw Ali, then he would have to see Sarah, too.

"Mike, this doesn't have to be difficult." She kept her loving gaze on Ali, not on him. "How does Sunday work for you? You can pick Ali up after church services."

"Church?" He wasn't going to be dragged to church again like Sarah had done the last few months before their breakup. He didn't doubt the presence of God. He just doubted the relevance. And the truth is, he wasn't a man to get all touchy-feely over something he couldn't touch or see. He didn't need it. "I'm not going to attend with you two."

She held up one hand as if to ward off his argument. Her voice as always was mild. "I said after the service. You two can go out to a nice lunch and have a great afternoon together."

Oh. He couldn't object to that. He straightened his shoulders and stared hard at a hairline crack in the concrete. "It's good of you to let me see him, Sarah."

"Please don't feel that way. I know you are a tremendous part of Ali's life, and you should be. He's alive because of you. He's here because of you. You saved him. Can't you see how grateful I am to you?"

Grateful, huh? He never would have guessed it from

the look on her face and the shadows in her eyes. Then again, Sarah Alpert had proven to him that he never had really known her. So it ought to come as no surprise not to be able to guess what was going on with her now. "Ali, you and me are hitting the pizza joint on Sunday. Deal?"

"Deal!" Ali's grin was back. "Pepperoni is my favorite."

"You don't think I know that?" Holding on to his emotions, Mike ruffled the boy's dark hair and winked. "Come tomorrow, you won't forget about me and leave church without me, right?"

"Nope. I cross my heart." Ali made a big cross with his free hand.

The lump in Mike's throat felt the size of a boulder and he turned away before it could get any bigger. He strode off to his truck, calling his goodbye to the boy over his shoulder.

Driving away from that little kid was the hardest thing he'd ever had to do. And Sarah, oh, Sarah. He was hurting more than he could measure and a whole lot more than he would ever admit. He climbed in behind the wheel and backed the truck out into the street.

Ali was waving wildly. Man, it had been great to see the little kid. Mike put the truck in gear and put his heart on neutral. There was Sarah with her furry cat cradled in her arms, looking sadder than he'd ever seen her.

Too bad he was past feeling. He would do what he always did so well—brokenhearted or not—he would carry on. He concentrated on the road until the red and blue blink of the lights had faded from his rearview.

* * *

"Sarah? Know what?"

"What?" Laughing, she climbed from her knees and pulled back his covers.

"Dr. Mike's gonna teach me basketball."

"Yes, I heard that somewhere before."

"Oh, from me!" Laughing, Ali dove onto his bed and snuggled in, warm in his flannel jammies.

"Yes, from you, silly." Her heart swelled. She loved being a foster mom. She prayed that the adoption would work out. She smoothed the covers and tucked the sheet into place. "There. All snug?"

"Yeah." Ali pulled his Texas bear onto the pillow next to him.

Dr. Mike. Would praises for the man ever end? Probably not. Sarah brushed Ali's dark bangs from his eyes. The twice-weekly phone calls had hardly fazed her, but now that Mike was back in town— She squeezed her eyes briefly shut. Although it might be hard for her, Mike was important to her boy. She would simply have to deal with it. Somehow.

She turned off the little bedside lamp. She prayed that no nightmares would haunt him tonight. "Sleep well, little one."

"I'm too happy to sleep."

"Then you just lie quietly and think about all the good things that happened today." That usually did the trick. Sarah followed the fall of light to the shadowed hallway.

"There were sure a lot." Ali sighed, sounding content. In the dark shadows of his cozy room, she saw him give his bear an extra squeeze.

Sweet boy.

"You're gonna stay close, right, Sarah?"

"Right. I'll be just out in the living room. Very close."

"Good."

She waited until his breathing slowed before she eased down the hall and into the light of the living room. Clean laundry tumbled out of the basket she had left on one of the couches. A stack of papers were on the coffee table, awaiting gold stars and smiley faces. She had so much to do, and where were her thoughts?

On Mike. His eyes had looked almost haunted. He had felt so emotionally remote—more than usual. Something had changed him. Something happened in the desert. Her stomach twisted up so tight she could barely breathe. She sank onto the couch cushion. He might not have a drop of affection left for her, but she could not pretend.

She cared. She would always care about Mike. He had been more than her fiancé. More than the man she wanted to build her dreams with. He had been her best friend. Her confidant. Her soul mate. She could not pretend that seeing him tonight hadn't shattered her.

Love was a powerful blessing. She pulled two of Ali's tube socks from the basket and rolled them neatly. She had fallen in love so easily with Mike at first sight. He had been playing Frisbee on the tree-shaded common between their college dormitories with his buddies. The dappled sunlight had found him like grace as he leaped into the air, all powerful man and determination. He snatched the blue disc out of the air and he may as well have been grabbing hold of her heart.

With the breeze in his dark blond hair and laughter in his hazel eyes, she had been rendered speechless. Her library books had slipped out of her hand. He had come to help her and the moment he smiled at her, the world felt right.

Nothing had been right without him. She had to admit that. It was why she had decided to become a foster mom. First with Carlos, who had gone back to his biological mother five months before Ali had come into her life. Maybe part of her decision to foster had been a deep need to fill the emptiness that Mike had left. It was as if her soul knew that no matter how happy her future may be, something would always be missing. Mike would be missing. She would never be completely whole without him.

It was time to face that. She pulled a T-shirt from the basket—an olive-green army shirt that Mike had given Ali—and folded it carefully. Seeing the past and feeling the broken pieces of her dreams with him was not good for her. He had chosen the army over her. He had wanted to be everyone else's hero but hers. That wound would never stop hurting.

After all this time, her feelings for him were just as strong, if a bit different. She pulled a towel from the laundry and gave it a shake. Clarence wandered in from the kitchen and gave her a rusty purr.

Her life had gone one way. Mike's had gone another.

It wasn't what she wanted. It wasn't what she had meant when she had asked him not to extend his tour of duty. She would pray on it tonight and she would trust that the Lord would show her the way.

He hefted the last box from the back of his truck onto his shoulder and hoofed it up the walk. The post was a family neighborhood. The windows up and down the street were squares of light against the pressing darkness, and the colorful glow of Christmas lights blazed joyfully. Only his windows were dark. He was the only house without a single Christmas decoration.

He kept his heart cool and his thoughts on the task at hand. If he wasn't so good at self-control, he would be thinking about Ali right now and remembering the fun they had putting up those strings of red and blue lights. If he wasn't a man who prided himself on his un-yielding self-discipline, he might be remembering how sad Sarah had looked when he drove away.

He shouldered the door open and stacked the box on top of the others. There. The stack was neat and tidy and relatively out of the way. He gave the door a slight boot, sending it gently closed. The faint light from the kitchen fell through the pass-through into the entry hall, casting just enough to see the empty rooms.

His furniture would come first thing Monday morning. For now, he was content enough just to have a real roof over his head and a place to call his own. After sharing a tent with half a dozen other doctors, this modest little home seemed a luxury.

The adoption papers he had carefully filled out were on the counter. He didn't look at them as he picked them up and ripped them carefully in half. Just like that, his hopes were gone.

Alone, he crossed to the refrigerator, refusing to listen to the hollow sound of his boots echoing in the empty house. There was no one for him to call. Most of his buddies were either in the Mid East or spending the first night home with their families.

He didn't mind so much. He'd gotten used to being alone. He yanked open the door and hauled out a can of flavored iced tea. He popped the top and took a long slow slurp. Another luxury. It didn't seem to hit the spot, though. Maybe because this last tour had put a hole in his soul. Staying connected to Ali had helped mask that some, but now—

Mike shook his head and set the can on the counter. He walked away into the darkness. Sarah was going to adopt him. How could he have guessed that? He thought she was the perfect foster mother—in spite of all their differences he had to be honest about that—but adopt him? Why? She had been set on having her own children, and soon. Wasn't that the reason she had set down her ultimatum? Why hadn't she found someone else to walk down the aisle with?

The memory of her shadowed eyes cut him in two. She had avoided looking directly at him. She had talked to him as little as possible. She didn't seem to care how ruthlessly she had hurt him.

He unrolled his sleeping bag with a hard shake. Yes,

that was his breath huffing in the silence. He pressed his hand to his forehead and took a few slow mouthfuls of air. What was he doing? Blaming Sarah wasn't going to change a thing. He didn't really think it was her fault to begin with.

She hadn't loved him enough, but he didn't blame her for that. Even through his bitterness, he could clearly see she always had the best of intentions. She was pure sweetness with her chocolate cupcakes for dessert and her living-room shelves stuffed with children's books. She didn't live in his world. She didn't understand what he was fighting for day in and day out. That wasn't her fault.

No, he was angry at himself because he still cared for her. That's what this anger was. It was distracting him from a whole lot of hurt. His anger was spent.

In the silence of the comfortable bedroom in the pleasant neighborhood on this safe army post, the silence threatened to suffocate him. He could still hear the distant pop of artillery, and beep of monitors from ICU. Exhaustion clung to him. He sank to his knees, alone and lost.

It was going to be a long night.

Chapter Four

Church may have brought her peace and refreshed her spirit, but it hadn't given her an easy answer. Sarah stopped her SUV outside the post's security entrance and gathered her papers from the front seat. She lowered her window and smiled to the strapping young soldier who approached her.

Once, she had known nearly everyone who had stood guard because she had visited Mike on post so frequently. Now a stranger in uniform squinted at her and the interior of her vehicle. So much had changed.

"Good afternoon." She handed the guard her papers and pass, squinting in the low sunlight. "I'm visiting Dr. Mike Montgomery."

"You're on the list. One moment." After a curt nod, the soldier marched to the booth and made a call. A pair of soldiers, one with a German shepherd and another with a mirror, walked the length of her vehicle. It was good they took such precautions in these uncertain times. Sarah's hand tightened on the steering wheel, thinking of all the men and women who sacrificed for this country.

She understood how much that sacrifice meant. It was more than service to one's country. It meant forsaking time with family and friends, with hobbies and pastimes, and even one's personal dreams to make others safe. She had always known that, but ever since she had met Ali, what soldiers did for their country and the world had taken on a whole new perspective.

"Good day, ma'am." The soldier waved her through, opening the checkpoint gate.

She thanked him, but she was thinking of Mike. She was thinking of all the good Mike had done and continued to do. She never should have forced him to choose between her and the army. She should have been more understanding when he wanted to go back.

Her cell rang. She grabbed the phone from the outside pocket of her shoulder bag and hit the speaker button. "Hello?"

"Sarah?" Mike's rich voice filled the passenger compartment.

Why did her heart sigh at the sound?

"Hi, Mike. I'm on my way." She prayed her voice was as calm as she wanted it to be. "I'm running a few minutes late. I'm sorry about that."

"No prob. Ali and I are shooting hoops. If you turn at the second left, you should—"

"I see you." Since she traveled at the slow speed limit, she was able to spot the towering basketball hoops and the busy court. She flipped closed her phone. Her gaze went straight to the tall, square-shouldered figure standing beside a little dark-haired boy dribbling a ball.

Every roll of the tires brought her closer to the man, and as his features came more into focus, so did the stirring in her soul. A stirring she could not deny.

"Sarah!" Ali raced up to her as she hiked around to the sidewalk. "I made ten whole baskets and I winned."

"That's because you are the best ballplayer I know." Seeing him made her heart warm, and she loved how bright he looked from hanging with Mike. But it was the man striding toward her, with the ball under one arm and the breeze ruffling his short hair that made her pulse catch.

Her foot hit the ground too soon, and the sudden jarring ricocheted up her leg. How could he still have that effect on her? She brushed her hair out of her eyes, but that only made her see him more clearly.

He had changed. Gone was his quick and easy smile, the one that made dimples bracket his mouth and his hazel eyes twinkle with mischief. It wasn't only because of their breakup. She knew there was more. It was as if something had taken a big bite out of his soul. Shadows haunted his eyes, shadows that faded when he looked at Ali.

"He's quite a ballplayer." Mike winked. "Ali, what do you say we have another rematch? I need to try to win next time. I have a reputation to protect."

Ali laughed, pure sunshine. "Not now, right? 'Cuz we still gotta do the promised thing."

"What promised thing?" She glanced at her watch. "I thought you boys would be done by five."

"Apparently not." Mike tossed the ball to Ali, who caught it easily. The man was looking everywhere but at her. "The kid knows how to work me."

"The best ones do." Her words sounded strained. Her stomach was clamping tight. She laid a hand on Ali's shoulder. She was definitely uncomfortable. The faster she could put some distance between her and Mike, the better. "Toss the ball back. It's time for us to go, sunshine."

"No, it's not." Ali, nothing if not persistent, gave her his best puppy-dog look.

How was she going to say no to that?

"I meant to call," Mike explained. "Ali and I got to talking and it seems like I promised that we would do a lot of things when I got back. And so that means I owe the kid. He seems to think I meant we would do all these things the minute I got back." Mike rubbed the back of his neck, the way he did when he was either nervous or contemplating a tricky problem.

She hated to think that she was a problem to him. She took a step back. "Hey, don't let me stand in your way. Give me a call when you need me to come pick him up."

"No, I'll drop him off." There was a hint of strain in his words.

"Maybe that would be better." She let the crisp wind blow through her, and she felt it clear to her bones. Being near Mike was never going to get easier, she realized. She loved him, she had a mountain of regrets, and she wanted what she could not have. There was nothing to do but to walk away. "Fine. Just give me a call."

"Wait!" Ali dashed after her, the ball rolled out of his arms and he grabbed her by the hand. He dug in his heels, trying to stop her. "Don't go, Sarah. It's gettin' dark."

"It's all right." She knelt to give him a hug. "You don't have to worry. You're not going to lose me, okay?"

"'Kay." Ali gulped.

"What's all this about?" Mike strode closer, hands on his hips, looking ready to protect and defend. He was definitely one of the good guys.

She was definitely still in love with him. She would have to deal with that. She rose, set her chin and faced him. The moment her eyes met his steely gaze, a sharp pain razored through her midsection. Longing, she realized, the wish for his love.

"Ali gets a little nervous in the dark. You didn't notice it when you were over stringing the lights, because he was home. It's to be expected." She paused, waiting for him to understand.

He nodded once, and sadness pinched in his eyes. Sympathy for Ali changed him. His iron defenses melted and there was the man she adored. Big hearted and concerned for everyone.

Ali took Sarah by the hand, and then grabbed one of Mike's. "Sarah can come, too. She can watch. I'm gonna skate good."

She watched Mike's throat work, and emotions played across his rugged face. "Maybe another night," she offered.

"No." Mike's answer was abrupt. "That's not good for me. I start back tomorrow."

"Surely you have leave coming."

"I had it. Didn't want to take it."

"But why not?"

He gave her a cool look. He had closed up.

"Fine, it's not my business. I didn't mean to pry." She blushed, helpless, realizing what she had done. "I'm concerned about you, Mike."

"That's not your right, Sarah. You gave that up."

"I know." She hated the pain that sounded thick in his voice. She knew Mike. He hid most real emotion, and so this hint of it was a sign of much greater pain.

She took a step back. Was it possible that he felt this way, too? That he was full of regret for how he handled things between them. That he was sorry they had broken up?

"Come with us, Sarah." Mike's voice dipped low. "I want to talk to you about this."

About Ali. Yes, she knew he was concerned about him. She had a few things to say, too. "Then I'll tag along with you boys."

"Goody." Ali's relief was visible. He clung to her, his need palpable.

He made it easy to love him. She let him cling to her, comforted that she was doing at least this one thing right. If only she could say the same with Mike.

He scooped the ball from the grass and loped after them. It felt familiar to have him nearby, to hear the beat of his gait and the rustle of his movements as he whisked open the backseat door and held it. Always a gentleman.

"Thanks." Longing filled her. She fought against it as she helped Ali with his car seat buckles. Memories rushed into her mind's eye—of how he always held the door for her, of how safe it felt to be held in his arms and how easily they used to laugh together over everything and nothing.

The buckle snapped into place, she backed up a step and longing rose up again. She was so close to Mike, she could see the gold flecks in his eyes and the texture of his day's growth on his jaw. He opened the front passenger door for her, like he used to. Love filled her like a rising tide, sweeping away the hurt and the regret.

Maybe there was hope after all.

"Sarah! Look!" Ali called from the side of the rink. He clutched the rail with both hands, grinning ear to ear. "I'm good."

"You're fantastic." Sarah laid her coat on the bench beside her, safely on the sidelines. Since it was supper time, the rink was quiet, which was perfect for a little boy learning to skate. "I'm so proud of you."

"Me, too!" Ali glanced over his shoulder at the wide expanse of glittering ice. "But I can't skate as good as Dr. Mike."

"Who can?" Speaking of which, where had the man gone? He had been right behind Ali the last time she looked.

A pair of skates dangled in front of her. She twisted around on the bench, already knowing it was Mike behind her. He towered over her, and the fall of light from the dome ceiling cast a glow over his head and shoulders. For a moment, he stood as if unguarded.

"No one said you could sit on the sidelines." He lowered the skates into her waiting hands. "I don't want to hear any excuses. I know you can skate."

"Only because you taught me." She smiled up at him. "I haven't been on the ice since the last time I came here with you."

"The New Year's Eve fund-raiser for Children of the Day." Mike gave a brief nod, warming to her, as if with the memory. "That was a good time."

"It was." A very good evening together.

She bent to yank off her suede boots, trying to forget those warm memories that were more than two years old. The Prairie Springs skating rink had hosted the charity's yearly fund-raising event. Mike had just returned from a year's duty overseas, and they had never been closer. He had a year left to serve, and she was planning their wedding. Finally. He was home to stay, having served his last deployment. Her dreams were within reach. She had waited for him since college and then, at thirty-three, she couldn't wait to be his wife and the mother of his children.

They had skated the rink hand in hand, heart to heart, soul to soul. Life had been so good that evening, knowing she would never spend another day eaten up with fear that the phone or doorbell would ring, bringing word that Mike had been killed in action.

"Dr. Mike! Look!" Ali made sure his hero was watching as he took one hand off the rail and sailed what had to be three inches. His free hand grasped the rail again. "I did good."

Mike's chuckle was like music. "You did great, buddy."

"Look! I gonna do it again." Ali waited until he had Mike's undivided attention.

She managed to keep the boy in sight as she slipped on the skates. Out of the corner of her eye she saw Mike's shoulder dip. He hesitated, frozen in place. Had he been about to help her? Had he thought better of it?

She felt his gaze on her as she drew her laces tight and tied them. Don't think of all this could mean, she warned herself. That he had remembered her shoe size. That he wanted her to join him and Ali. That he had been almost ready to reach out to her.

No, reading too much into this could be disastrous. Her heart had been totally broken. She didn't want to risk more heartache. She straightened, the rental skates heavy on her feet. His nearness made her shiver with hope. The warm brush of his hand at her nape was as familiar as her own breath.

"He's quite an athlete."

Her senses scrambled. Ali. Mike was talking about Ali. She set her chin and cleared her throat. Her mind was nothing but fuzz. "He's a very active little boy. It's a blessing, after all he's been through."

"I almost agree with you."

"Almost?"

"I'm no religious man, but sometimes—" He shook his head. "Sometimes you want to believe in something. He's waiting for us."

Ali. Right. Sarah wobbled on the narrow skate blades. When she took her first step, she prayed she looked completely normal. Totally unaffected. But how could she be? With every step she took, Mike was right behind her. The pad of his gait was a welcome sound straight out of her memories. The power of his reassuring presence was like waltzing with her dreams.

"Dr. Mike! Sarah!" Ali skidded a few feet, holding on tight all the way. "You can skate, too, Sarah?"

"I don't know. It's been a long time. You may have to help me."

"Hold on to me, Sarah."

It helped to focus her attentions on her foster son, the little boy she loved so dearly. The fuzz cleared and the ache of longing stilled as she took Ali's outstretched hand in her own. "Thanks, sweetie. Look how good you're doing!"

"I know. Look." Ali let go of the bar and for a second he was wobbling on his own. She made sure to keep him as steady as she could until he grabbed the bar, still upright. So pleased with himself. "Whew. That was a long time."

"The longest." A movement caught her attention. Mike gliding to Ali's other side. He looked at home on skates, easily athletic, as he had always been.

"Let's teach him together." It was as if time had looped backward to that long-ago day when they had been happy and in love. The shadows had vanished from his eyes and the harsh lines from his face and he looked as free and as at peace as he had that day. "Are you ready for your first lesson, Ali?"

"Yes, sir!" He tipped his head back. Sarah gave thanks that the boy was healthy and relatively happy. He was a resilient little guy. Anyone watching him would not guess how hard the nights were for him or how deeply he grieved the family he had lost.

"Look. We're way out on the ice." He sounded so proud of himself.

It was actually a few feet, but to a little boy it was a long way. Sarah worked to keep her thin blades balanced. She hadn't been on the ice in a long time and it showed. "I don't know about you, Ali, but I'm starting to miss the wall."

"I'm not!" Ali held tight, secure between them. "I wanna go fast. Can we, Dr. Mike?"

Mike chuckled. "You're askin' me because you figure of the two of us, I'll be the one to say yes."

"Ye-ah." Ali dragged out the word, his eyes rolling upward as he thought. "But I still wanna go fast. Like him."

A teenaged skater whizzed by.

"Ready?" Mike was saying to the boy. "Just scoot your right skate forward. C'mon, give it a try."

Sarah dug in with her left skate, keeping her place in the ice as Ali hesitated. He gulped and stared down hard at his toes. She dug in with her tip, waiting for him to gather his pluck and take that first startling slide into the expanse of the ice. Whatever happened, she was going to hold him steady. She would make sure he didn't fall. It felt good knowing the man on Ali's other side felt the same way.

Mike didn't have to say it—it was in his stance, protective and strong. It was in his steady patience as he waited for Ali to shift his weight on his skates. For a moment the boy wobbled and then his left skate went back as his right skate went forward.

She moved and Mike moved and together they kept him upright, flawlessly. Safe and secure, he was laughing. "I'm skating fast!"

"You sure are, buddy." Mike's rumbling chuckle was the dearest sound to her. Still.

Sarah tried to keep her eyes focused clearly on Ali as he scooted his left skate forward, in danger of each skate going a different way. But as she pushed off to keep up with him and used her toe pick to stop and hold him steady, she saw the faint image of her lost dreams so clearly. Maybe her lost hopes were not gone, after all.

"Right foot." Mike's amused instruction was punctuated with his low rumbling chuckles. "That's it. You're gettin' it, buddy. Left foot. Right foot."

"Good job, Ali." Sarah cheered as they turned a shaky corner. The length of the ice rink spread out before them, glossed with light and shimmering as if with hope. There were the remembrances of her dreams, images she could see once again. Of how she had once envisioned being with Mike, teaching their son to skate one day, just like this, side by side with a child between them. With love between them.

Did Mike feel this way, too?

"We can make it all the way to the wall down there, don't you think, buddy?" Mike's confidence was tempered by his affection for the boy. The man she loved so much looked transformed, as if he could see his buried hopes.

"Y-yeah." Ali clearly tried to be as confident. "I'm a good skater."

"Yes you are." Her voice was thick and laced with emotion, but she didn't bother to hide it. Adoring the boy, adoring the man, she held on tight. Patiently she skated one choppy glide at a time, her heart so full it hurt.

Chapter Five

For a while there, Mike had almost forgotten that the last year had passed. As they skated like the amateurs they were around the public rink, he had almost forgotten that the woman laughing with him was the same one who had devastated him. Now, as he took a bite of the pizza, he took a good look at the woman who had torn him apart.

She sat across from him, looking as pretty as ever, with the fall of light on her red hair and flawless complexion. She took a napkin from the dispenser on the table and gave Ali's face a few swipes.

"Sarah!" The boy protested. "I like pepperoni juice."

"But you're wearing it." She bit her soft bottom lip to keep from laughing. Love radiated from her. It was plain to see that the match was as good for her as for Ali. She was one lucky lady, getting to love and raise the boy.

He knew there was no place for him in their new family.

You promised me, Mike. He could hear the pain vibrating in her voice crisp and touching in his memory. *You said this was your last tour. That you were getting out.*

That's what I thought, but I was wrong. In memory, too, he could still feel the conviction of his words and the weight of his decision. *There are still threats to our country, and this is my duty, Sarah. I serve the men and women who put their lives on the line for our freedom.*

But she hadn't heard him. She hadn't understood. He had always suspected that it was because she hadn't wanted to. She wanted her way. He wanted everything with her. That is, until he saw the real Sarah Alpert. The woman who hadn't loved him enough to wait. She hadn't even bothered to come see him off. To say goodbye.

Pain cut through him. He winced and set down his half-eaten slice of pizza onto the plate in front of him. That was something he couldn't deny or ignore. Bitterness spilled across his tongue, sour and relentless. She hadn't cared about him, not down deep. It had nearly killed him to board that bird and leave her behind.

She obviously hadn't felt the same way.

"Mike, are you all right?"

He blinked, bringing the room back into focus. He was in the present again with the agony of that tough day. Somehow he had to get his defenses up and his heart walled off or he would be vulnerable to that sweet concern on her face. The most beautiful face he had ever seen.

"Sure. You know how I feel about pizza." It was an old joke between them.

She turned her attention to him, sitting there with her

perfect posture. When their gazes met, his heart flat lined.

It was the wrong thing to say.

Seconds passed, and he didn't know how to break the silence. If he knew what to say, then he could make light of how he always used to say that pizza was his favorite thing on earth, next to Sarah's smile.

"I need more." Ali picked up his plate and presented it. "Please."

"More?" It was easier to joke. He shook his head. "Nope. No more for you, mister."

"But I'm hungry." Ali grinned, stifling a giggle. "And there's lots left."

"Sure, but it's all for me."

"No." Ali giggled. "It's for me and Sarah, too. You're supposed to share, Dr. Mike. Sarah says so."

"Well, if Sarah says." He rolled his eyes, earning another laugh from his favorite buddy and grabbed the pie server. "What piece do you want?"

"The biggest!" Ali leaned against the table and studied the pizza tray. "Wait. The biggest one with the most pepperonis."

"That would be this one." He served it. "There you go. Sarah? How about you?"

"I'll take that small one, if you don't mind." She scooted her plate toward him, and he kept his gaze down. Maybe if he could avoid looking at her, he could keep the memories down where they belonged and all the unwanted feelings with them.

The trouble was, as he slid the smallest piece onto

her plate, she was still in his field of sight. The delicate line of her hands, the splash of her reflection in the window beside him and the dulcet lull of her voice as she spoke with Ali.

"Thanks, Mike."

"Sure." He took another piece for himself. Whatever happened, he could not start letting himself think of what might have been. What he had to focus on was why he was here. He had to let Ali go, and he needed Sarah's help to do it.

"Mike?"

He blinked, realizing too late that she had asked him a question. "Sorry, I missed that."

"I asked if you were settled in to your new place."

"Getting there." He took a sip of root beer. He was no longer hungry. He didn't want to make small talk with Sarah. No, that's not what he wanted at all.

"Dr. Mike?" Ali was working on that big piece of pizza and making good progress. "What are we gonna do now?"

"Now?" He put down his glass. "You think there's more to do?"

"You said lots. Remember?" Ali bounced up onto his knees on the booth cushion. "You said football. You said I could come see you at work. You said about a Christmas tree. You said I would have a room, too."

"You remember all that?"

"Yep. I remember really good."

"I'll say." He shook his head, a smile tugging the corners of his mouth. "I promised to do all that with you?"

"No." Ali pulled a pepperoni disc off his pizza slice. "You promised lots more."

"You are in big trouble, Mike."

"So I see." He braced himself but nothing could prepare him for the impact of Sarah's smile. It was as if she had reached inside and touched his soul.

Uncomfortable, he looked away, but nothing could diminish the feeling that the rift between them had changed.

"Dr. Mike." Ali tromped through the front doors of the pizza parlor and onto the twilight sidewalk. "You're comin' for hot chocolate, right?"

Sarah swept past Mike, who held the door open for her, waiting for his answer. Tonight had been confusing. On one hand he had scarcely looked at her. He had been withdrawn. And on the other, there were moments that had felt like old times when they had laughed together and everything between them felt effortless.

What was Mike going to say to Ali? She stepped out into the cool night and drew her coat tight around her. Was their evening going to continue? "It's early, Mike. You might as well."

"No, I have things to get done." The shadows seemed darker around him as he joined them. He seemed darker. "Sorry, buddy. I'll have to pass on the cocoa."

"How about with lots of marshmallows?"

"Nope, I just can't."

"Why, Mike?" Ali skipped to his hero and clung to his hand.

"I've got to get laundry done if I want clean clothes to wear to work tomorrow." Mike didn't look happy turning the boy down.

Of course not. Sarah padded after them on the sidewalk. The man and boy had an undeniable bond. Maybe this situation didn't need to be so awkward. She caught sight of their reflection in the candy store's window. With the man and little boy hand in hand and her a pace behind, they looked like a family to any passersby.

A family. Her step faltered. Emotion gathered within her as she forced herself to keep up with the quick-walking duo. Isn't that what she had been praying for so hard and for so long? It was as if her dreams were coming back to life.

"Guess this is where we part ways." Mike halted between two vehicles parked side by side, her SUV and his truck. "It was great spending time with you, buddy. You be good tonight for Sarah, ya hear?"

Ali grinned.

"You've got that right." She couldn't help ruffling his hair, sweet baby.

He laughed, taking her hand and holding on tight. "Are you sure you don't want cocoa, Dr. Mike? It's real yummy."

"I'm sure it is." Mike's sadness was obvious, even in the shadows, even in the night's darkness. The flash of Christmas lights did not seem to touch him as he wandered between the vehicles.

He was waiting for her to unlock the passenger door, so she hit the remote. The locks popped.

Sure enough, Mike opened the door. "Up you go, kid."

Ali's delight was tangible as he was lifted into the air, turned upside down and then gently torpedoed into the backseat. His laughter was a cherished sound.

Maybe it was simply the golden glow from the overhead Christmas star adorning a lamppost, but joy filled her. She had to hope, no, she had to believe, that God had a plan for all of them.

"There. You buckled up safe?"

"Yes, sir!" Ali's voice was muffled from inside the vehicle, but nothing could muffle his enthusiasm. "About that cocoa—"

Mike laughed, deep and tender and kind. Always a good man. Why hadn't she seen that before? Even when he was wanting to put off their wedding one more time, she should have known. She should have trusted him. She should never have let him go.

"If you're trying to wear me down about coming over tonight, it's not gonna happen." Amused, he grabbed the door, getting ready to close it. He hesitated, and no darkness or shadow could hide the affection on his face.

He really loves Ali. The realization sent tingles down her spine. She knew Mike cared about him, but to see his secret revealed—a father's love—made her hope all the harder.

"Good night, buddy."

"'Night, Dr. Mike. You gonna call me tomorrow?"

"I'll call you tomorrow." He closed the door.

Hope. It twinkled through her like the tiny lights

threaded through the shrubbery. It chased away the darkness like the moon in the sky. She wished to know the shelter of Mike's arms again, to lay her cheek against his iron-strong chest and hear the reliable rhythm of his heartbeat. She had been without him for so long—without his laughter, without his friendship and without his tenderness. Every fiber of her being ached to fix what was broken between them.

"Sarah." Mike said her name without cold gruffness or stoic indifference. No, her name on his lips was a sweet promise. He opened her door and held it for her. "We need to talk."

"Yes, we do." She had much to say to him and a basketful of regrets. As she slid into the seat and he closed her door, she thought she saw regret in his eyes, too.

It was enough to give her the courage she needed. What she had to say wouldn't be easy. She started the engine and drove off, leaving him behind in the gathering darkness.

"Is now a good time?"

Sarah looked up from her desk at Prairie Springs Elementary School to see Mike standing in her classroom doorway, military straight and soldier strong. Her chicken salad sandwich forgotten, she hopped to her feet. Days had passed without the two of them speaking. Both times he had called Ali, the boy had been waiting by the phone. He had learned to recognize Mike's number on the caller ID box. She had waited nearby each time, but Ali had hung up the phone after saying goodbye.

"I had wondered if you'd forgotten." She yearned for

his embrace. She ached to be drawn close in his arms and sigh against his chest. Missing him was like an unhealed wound. But he held back in the doorway.

This must be hard for him, too. Of course it would be. She thought of all the distance between them, of all the time that had passed.

"Now is a perfect time." She took a tentative step toward him. Her low heels tapping on the floor was the only sound as their eyes met.

As if he had been slapped, he jerked away, took a step into the room and glanced around. He could have been a stranger. "Nice job."

"I try." They both knew how hard she worked on her bulletin boards—always had, always would. The green board with the candy-cane forest and snowman family carrying gifts. The gold-papered board with the Christmas tree-shaped calendar, brightly decorated with paper ornaments and yarn garlands.

Did Mike remember all the evenings he would sit studying his medical books or journals while she cut and clipped, colored and pasted? She didn't know how to ask him, and because her knees were shaking, she sat on the edge of her desk. Did he miss the way it used to be?

"This is your best one yet. Or, at least the best I've seen." He jammed his hands into his pockets. The leather bomber jacket he wore suited him, masculine and casual with a hint of wear.

"Thanks. You didn't come all this way to talk about my artwork."

"No. I haven't." He marched into the room, all business, unreadable. "It's about Ali."

"Oh." It wasn't what she expected. It wasn't the subject that had kept her up late at night with her mind spinning out all the possible ways to tell him—as well as all the possible ways it could go wrong. "Ali had a great time with you on Sunday."

"So did I." Mike stared around the room at the little desks grouped in a circle, at the wide windows offering views of the wind-swept playground and finally at the tiles in front of her shoes.

But not at her. He kept his gaze shielded from her. His chiseled face was a mask of stone. Mike was, as always, the epitome of self-control. She clasped her hands together and waited. She prayed for guidance to handle whatever he had come to say.

"The thing is, I need your help." Mike appeared uncomfortable. Tension gripped his jaw. His shoulders were a rigid, hard line.

"Of course I'll help you." She would move mountains for him. "This is about Ali?"

"Yep. You have him, Sarah, and that's the way it ought to be." He pulled his hands out of his jacket pockets and stared at them. He seemed to be wrestling with something. "Thanks for letting me take Ali on Sunday. I know it wasn't easy for you. It wasn't easy for me."

"I'm sorry about that." Her hand shook as she smoothed a wrinkle in her skirt. "I'm sorry about a lot of things."

"I wish things had been different, too, but they

aren't." Was he angry or sad? She couldn't tell, but he went on talking. "What matters is Ali. It means a lot that I could spend time with him."

"Of course you can see him. You saved his life. You've been his anchor, a father figure. Your interest has made an enormous difference to his welfare. Mike, you called him twice a week since he left your MASH unit months and months ago. You have been the one steady adult male influence in his life. I hope you don't pull away from him because of me."

Silence was her only answer. Mike always kept his feelings to himself—those few he would allow himself. He was mad at her. She had said too much.

No, she realized. She had hit on exactly what he had come to do. "You're going to stop seeing him?"

"What choice do I have?" His tone was even and steady. "I had it all planned out. First thing I did when I set foot on U.S. soil was to fill out adoption papers."

"Adoption papers?" She halted. Had she heard him right?

"I decided to adopt Ali, but you beat me to it."

Adopt Ali? Those two words collided in her brain, and she couldn't think past them. "What? Oh, Mike, I didn't know."

"I know." His answer was curt but not harsh. He cleared his throat sounding indifferent, but she knew he wasn't. "Ali's better off with you, Sarah. You have more to give him than I ever could."

"I don't know about that. Now that I've seen you with him, I—" Her throat closed and she took off toward the window, staring at the blur of the monkey bars through the rain-smeared glass. "I love him. I've been afraid something like this would come along and I'd have to g-give him up. That's what happened to the first child I fostered. I wanted to adopt little Carlos, but he went back to his family. It tore me apart."

"Sarah, I don't want that for you or Ali." His voice dipped tenderly. His strong, healing hands curved over her shoulders, comforting her just like he used to do. Just for a moment, before he stepped back and away from her. "I can't think of a better parent for him."

"But if you wanted him?"

"You were here, Sarah. You were here with him. You saw him through his surgery. You made a home for him. Because of you, he has a safe, happy environment in which to recover and grow." Tenderness warmed his hazel eyes. "You're what he needs, Sarah. I'm not. I can see that now. I have the army."

And there it was, the conflict that had driven them apart. The army came first and foremost to Mike and she believed it always would. Although now she had come to understand something new. "Your commitment to the military is not a bad thing, Mike. It's a very, very good one."

"*What?* I can't believe my ears. This, coming from you?" One eyebrow quirked up over pain-shot eyes. "You make it sound like a compliment."

"I know, that's a change for me."

"I'll say."

She needed a few feet of distance to find the right

words. She had so much to say. The last year had changed her in countless ways. "I've had a chance to see the results of the work you do firsthand."

"Ali?"

"Yes, and Whitney Harpswell. She's back home in part because of you." Could he see how much she admired him? Was too much showing on her face? "It's important work, Mike. No one is more committed than you, and I see now why. You save lives. You save other people's loved ones. I have a foster son because of your dedication."

"It's not what you think." He looked in anguish.

Poor Mike. How many men and women were alive because of him? "You should see Ali as much as you like. He needs you, too."

For one brief moment, his gaze met hers. It was as if he could see into her thoughts, as impossible as that was. For one brief moment, tenderness filled his eyes. Hope lurched within her before he tore away.

"That's just the thing." Mike seemed distant again. "I need your help to ease out of his life. He's more dependent than I thought."

Oh. If she hadn't known him, then she would have missed the grief hugging the deeper tones of his words. "I thought you loved him."

"I do." He didn't show an ounce of emotion; he didn't even blink. This was the Mike she knew, stoic, steely and able to keep his distance. He cleared his throat. "I don't want to hurt the little guy. Will you help me?"

"How can I? You want to cut him out of your life?"

She thought of the man and boy in her backyard kicking the soccer ball around, their laughter punctuating the crisp, wintry air. She thought of how his eyes had darkened when he confessed he had wanted to adopt Ali. "I don't think it is right for either one of you."

"Then do you have a better solution?"

"Yes." The answer came to her quietly, like a gentle loving whisper. She searched his face. The squint of tension around his eyes, the tendons tight in his neck made her think there was a deeper reason why this was hard for him.

Fear quaked through her. She reached out for him and laid her hand flat on his chest. The thump of his heart vibrated against her palm. Like lightning cracking from the sky to the earth, so did the connection from her heart to his. She could feel his anguish. He was hurting, too.

There was a way for them both to stop hurting, a way for this heartache to end.

"M-Mike?" His name trembled on her lips and echoed in the chambers of her soul. "I have so very many regrets. I wish I could go back and change what I said to you and how I said it."

A muscle twitched in his tight jaw, the only hint that he was feeling something uncontrollable. The corners of his mouth softened, and this was also the Mike she knew, compassionate and tender.

"I still love you." She was no longer trembling, for she was speaking the truth. Standing out on a limb, fearing she might fall and praying Mike would catch her. "Say you still love me, too. Please, can you forgive me?"

Chapter Six

"Forgive you?" Mike couldn't believe what his ears were telling him. His heart hardened. He plainly heard the emotion, thin and tremulous in her voice. Her regrets and apologies were echoed on her face. The pain he saw there could bring him to his knees.

He couldn't let it. He couldn't forget what she had done to him. Maybe he didn't want to. He closed his eyes, hoping she would not see the truth, hoping that she would never know how much she had hurt him. It would make him too vulnerable. Already her hand on his chest was drawing up tender feelings.

He dug deep for all the anguish he'd been through, all the sleepless nights, all the running from the pain and the agony when he couldn't run anymore. She thought her fair-weather level of love was all right now? That he could forgive the fourteen years she had been the love of his life?

He took a deep breath and stepped away from her

touch. She hadn't loved him enough, and he was only doing the right thing in walking away. In letting her know exactly what she had done to him. He sharpened his words, gathered up his verbal weapons and opened his mouth only to find there were none. He couldn't do it. As bitter as he was, he couldn't say a single word to hurt her.

By the looks of things, she was hurting enough. Tears stood pooled in her eyes, vibrant and full of sorrow. She appeared so unhappy, that tore his heart out, too.

"I'm sorry." The words came out gently, with the love he used to feel for her. With the tenderness she had once rejected. "You were the one who didn't want me, remember?"

"That's not what I meant, Mike. I've always wanted you. I've always loved you." Those tears trembled, ready to fall. She fought them back. "Can't you see that I was afraid to lose you?"

"No. You *did* lose me."

"I wanted you to commit to me, Mike, that's all—"

"I can't do this." Her pain was everywhere, on her face, in his soul and in the very air between them. "It's over, Sarah. It was over when I learned the truth about you. I never should have trusted you."

"Truth? What truth?" She stared up at him wide-eyed, full of confusion and even as the first tear fell, it was her sweetness he saw. She had never meant to hurt him.

Just as he never meant to hurt her. He grimaced, wishing he knew how to say the right thing, but there was nothing to fix this and even less to heal it. This is what love came to in the end—nothing but pain.

"Come here, Sarah."

She had turned away, trying to hide her heartbreak, bucking up her chin the way she always did, blinking hard, gasping for air trying to stall the oncoming sobs. That broke him, too.

He couldn't feel the hurt or the tenderness as he caught her by the curve of her shoulder to turn her toward him. He'd been right. One lone tear tracked down her porcelain cheek. He rubbed it away with the pad of his thumb, refusing to feel the warm silk of her skin and the tearing of his soul.

"We can't go back." He hated it. "Maybe you and I were never meant to be. Could be that's why it never worked out between us."

"You can't believe that."

He could see that she didn't. He sure hoped the defenses would hold, because he hated seeing her like this, hurting, when there wasn't a thing he could do about it. "All we can do is go forward. You and I have to do what's right for that little boy in your care."

"That's what I'm doing."

"I know." He could see she was becoming defensive. Of course he could see that. "No one could be better for Ali than you."

"I don't know about that. What about you?"

"No, not me." He'd wanted the job of raising the kid, but he'd lost out on that. "I want Ali to have the best, and that's you."

"If that's what you think, then why can't we—"

"No. We can't. Don't go there, Sarah." He didn't know what she had been about to say, but he didn't like the "we" part. Wherever it had been going, it would only bring more agony to both of them. He took a step away, putting distance between them, drawing back his caring and shoring up his defenses. It wasn't easy to walk away from a dream, because that's what Sarah was to him. Always had been, would always be.

"All right." She turned away from him to stare back out the window. The first round of lunch must be over, because there were little kids outside running around squealing and climbing on the bars. Her shoulders were set straight and strong, but vulnerability clung to her.

Maybe it was just his wishful thinking. Maybe it was the tear still damp on his thumb. Either way, Mike couldn't let himself think of her crying after he stepped foot out the door. He had to be cool and rational and do the best thing for the boy and for Sarah, too.

"I'll do as you ask." Her words sounded hollow, as if she were putting up her defenses, too. "You're right. We have to make this adjustment as easy as we can for Ali."

"Thanks, Sarah. That's a big relief. I don't want to hurt him."

"I know." She swallowed hard and crossed her arms around her middle. "This is going to be hard for him. He's lost everyone else."

"I know, but he has you." He made it sound like a compliment.

She wasn't fooled. Mike had never felt that way about her, not truly. Or at least it was easier to believe he hadn't. Otherwise how could she hold herself together as she listened to the strike of his boots on the tile floor? How could she keep the tears at bay as he paused near the doorway? She could picture him, turning toward her one last time, the apology on his handsome face and the shadows in his eyes.

She would never know what happened to him over there. She would never know a lot of things, and she hated that she still loved him as he broke the silence between them.

"Goodbye, Sarah. Take care of yourself."

"You, too, Mike." The words came out rough, and she wished she was strong enough to keep the tears out of her voice. She wasn't.

She listened to the knell of his gait heading down the hall, growing distant until she could no longer hear him. Goodbye hovered on her lips, unspoken. She could not say the word. It made it easier to set her chin, gather her dignity and head back to her desk, even as her vision blurred.

"Sarah, are you all right?"

She looked up, realizing she was walking out of the school building on autopilot, and walking by one of her best friends. Sally Winthrop, first-grade teacher and fellow church member, looked concerned as she stood holding the door open to the crisp, breezy outdoors.

"I'll be all right." That was the truth. And as long as she didn't think about Mike or say his name, she could stay numb enough to hold it together. Why had she thought that he would love her enough now? He loved the army. While she no longer blamed him for it, it still hurt. Badly.

"Did I see Mike walking down the hall during lunch?"

Sarah did her best not to wince at the sound of Mike's name. She could handle this. She could. "Y-yes. He dropped by to talk about Ali."

"That has to be a sticky situation, with the two of them being close." All kind sympathy, that was Sally. "How are you holding up?"

"I'm holding." That was the truth, too. She had to handle this. She couldn't fall apart. Ali needed her to handle this the right way. So did Mike. She had seen the anguish on his face when she had told him she still loved him. Anguish, when she had suspected he might still love her, too. How could she have been so wrong? "It's tough seeing Mike again, but Ali is worth it."

"Have you heard anything more about your adoption petition?"

"No, but at this stage no news is good news, or so I'm told." Sarah breezed outside and into the cold, struggling to put a smile on her face. There was no need to worry Sally. "How did things with your problem child turn out?"

"He was a perfect angel today." Sally shook her head, scattering her tidy blond curls, as she fell in beside Sarah on the sidewalk. A serious wind battered the bare branches overhead. "Kids. You've got to love 'em. They sure keep us on our toes."

"They do." She pulled her keys from her pocket, wistfully admiring the life her friend had. Sally had three kids—two girls and a boy—and an adoring, devoted husband. Sarah and Sally were the same age. Sarah knew it was wrong to compare herself with her friend, God had a different plan in mind for everyone. She simply wanted a family life so badly, one full of love and laughter and happiness.

"I would love to chat with you, but I've got my kids waiting for me to pick them up."

"I have Ali waiting at the church day care, too." Since he wasn't in her afternoon session.

"I'll see you bright and early." Sally smiled as she stopped next to her minivan. "Good luck with the Mike situation."

"I need it. Thanks." More than Sally knew. Sarah gave her remote a push. Her locks popped and she pulled open her door. She had a dozen things needing her attention—the press announcements to drop by the newspaper office for the Children of the Day fundraiser, a quick stop to pick up a few of Ali's Christmas gifts that had come in on order and a vase of flowers to take to Whitney Harpswell's hospital room. But where did her mind go? To Mike, always to Mike.

She could feel his hands on her shoulders, comforting her. She could still hear the kind timbre of his voice. *Maybe you and I were never meant to be. Could be that's why it never worked out between us.*

Rationally, she knew maybe he was right. As hard as it was to admit. But as she dropped behind the wheel and settled her bags on the passenger seat, all the love in her heart cried out, no. No, it couldn't be. Fourteen years of one's life should not be a waste.

She had spent precious years of her life with him, all of her twenties and part of her thirties. Looking forward to her phone ringing and the delight of hearing his voice. Of not being able to wait for the day to end so they could be together over dinner, either at his place or hers, making a meal together and then talking over their day.

She missed being able to turn to him when she needed comfort and caring. She missed being able to tell him everything and having him do the same. She missed the way he would tell a story out of the most ordinary circumstances, but in a way sure to make her laugh. All the time she had spent terrified for him when he was deployed. All the time her soul felt brighter knowing that he loved her.

All of that was gone. Forever gone. Mike had said it best: *All we can do is go forward.*

She would go her way. He would go his. He would find someone else to date and love and marry. Some other lucky woman to cook with and laugh with and raise kids with. He would be happy—because she would pray that he was so every day of her life to come.

But how could she be? Without him, without Mike, her future was bleak. Her heart could not imagine loving any other man. Not one.

She might not be the love of Mike's life, but he was the love of hers.

She sorted through her keys, fighting tears, fighting to keep hold of the numbness. She thought of Ali. He had an appointment late this afternoon at the church's grief center. The last thing she wanted was for him to be late to that.

She started the engine and blinked until the world came back into focus. She put the vehicle in gear and drove off, as if today was like any other day.

The tears in Sarah's eyes haunted Mike. Through the afternoon, he fought to stay distant. He fought to stay unaffected. Not even his defenses could handle the strain. *I still love you. Say you still love me, too. Please, can you forgive me?* Her vulnerable, heartfelt declaration had hit him like a cluster bomb, fragmenting the cool control he prided himself on.

Don't think about Sarah. He pulled into his driveway and into the garage. He wished he could shut off his thoughts as easily as the truck's engine. He pocketed his keys, grabbed his gym bag and the two plastic grocery sacks from the back and hiked into the house.

Empty. His steps, his movements and the rustle of the bags settling on the countertop echoed in the empty rooms. He pulled out the plastic containers of potato salad and rotisserie chicken. After washing his hands, he pulled a knife from the drawer and got right to work slicing vegetables and bread and chicken. The lonesomeness pressed on him like the ocean on a submarine.

I've always loved you. Can't you see that I was afraid to lose you? Sarah's voice resounded in his head. He forced it to silence right along with the ache echoing within him. She hadn't loved him enough then; she certainly didn't love him enough now. She was lonely; that was all. And so was he.

Within minutes he had a salad bowl filled and a dinner plate reheating in the microwave. He poured a glassful of juice and carried everything past the table into the living room. He had a TV tray set up in front of the television. With a click of the remote the screen blazed to life, chasing away the silence.

He stabbed into his salad, spearing a cucumber and lettuce. Why couldn't he get rid of the emotion sitting behind his sternum? Best not to think about why. It probably had something to do with the woman he refused to think about. He was over her. He was not in love with her. So what could it be?

Scar tissue, that's what. Some wounds never healed right. Some wounds, no matter how skilled the surgeon or how well mended, hurt now and then. He figured seeing Sarah again was going to hurt. He knew now he'd been right—and the only solution was the right one. He didn't plan on seeing her again.

His cell chirped, not his pager. Since he was on call tonight, he gave a sigh of relief before he tugged his phone out of his back pocket. Fellow surgeon Tom Beck's name was on the call screen. Mike had nothing but respect for his friend and colleague. They had served together overseas. Tom might be young, but he had a steady hand and a calm manner even when bullets were zipping through the O.R. He answered. "What's up, Tom?"

"Hey, Major. Some of the guys are on for a basket-ball game down at the gym. Old-timers versus residents."

"Old-timers?" The last time he had looked, thirty-six wasn't close to old. "I'm offended, Tom."

Tom had an easy laugh. "Hey, I didn't come up with the term. How about long-timers?"

"Fine. Count me in." Maybe that's what he needed to shake this off, a good, hard workout. "When and where?"

"Gym down at the rec center seven o'clock. Guess what I did?"

He could tell by the sheer happiness in the sergeant's voice that he had popped the question to his long-time girl. "You didn't. I thought you were smarter than that, Tom."

"What are you talking about? I'm smart enough to know what I've got. She said yes, too. I'm officially an engaged man."

"Congratulations." Maybe things would go easier for Tom. "She's a lucky lady."

"Believe me, I'm the lucky one."

Mike remembered feeling the same way. He had proposed to Sarah almost five years ago now. He had surprised her by going down on one knee when they were decorating the Christmas tree in her little yellow house. She had just closed on it and been so excited to put up the tree for the first time that she hadn't realized what he had been doing at first.

In his mind's eye he could still see her aglow from the tree lights and the happy shock on her face. He had been pretty happy then, too.

Sad, how things changed.

* * *

One day passed and then another. As Sarah cradled a bouquet of flowers in one hand and clutched Ali's hand with the other, she had to admit her emotional wounds were not getting any better. As they stepped through the hospital's automatic doors, she braced herself. She knew what was coming. Now, after she had humiliated herself so completely with her declaration of love to Mike, any mention of him stung.

"When's Dr. Mike gonna call? It's been long." Ali glanced around the crowded entry area. "Do you think he's here?"

"No. And as for him calling you, what did I tell you?" Gently, Sarah nudged him toward the bank of elevators.

"Uh, that I'm s'posed to wait?"

"That's right." She pressed the call button.

"But waiting is hard." Ali flashed his dimple, quite aware she thought he was the most adorable little boy ever.

"Yes, but you have to think of Mike. He's awful busy. I'm sure he was just as busy when you were hanging out with him in the MASH unit."

"Yep, he was really busy." Ali gave a heavy, disappointed sigh. "He worked and worked. I couldn't even see him."

"It's probably like that now." She hated that this was hurting Ali. What was the solution? Seeing Mike hurt her, and he didn't want to see her. He was right about there only being one solution. Mike was going to ease away from Ali. What other choice did they have?

The doors slid open. Ali marched into the empty elevator. "Can I hit the number? Can I, Sarah?"

"Yes." She gave him the floor number and watched over him to make sure he picked the right one. "Good boy. You are a smarty."

"Not as smart as Dr. Mike."

Sarah rolled her eyes. This is how it had been going over the last two days. Ali's requests for his favorite doctor had gone up right along with his number of nightmares. Poor boy. She ruffled his hair, her throat too tight to say what she felt. The doors eased shut and the elevator lifted, chugging upward to a slow stop.

"I like escalators better," Ali informed her as he tugged her into the corridor. "Know what, Sarah?"

"What?" The chances were one hundred percent it would be about Mike.

"I know what. I colored a picture for Dr. Mike."

"You did?"

"He's gotta see it."

Fortunately they were approaching the nurse's station and she didn't have to say more on the subject of Mike Montgomery.

After leaving Ali with Lily, who was the mother of one of her afternoon kindergarten students, Sarah took the flowers down the hall. Whitney Harpswell had a private room. A soldier from the Prairie Springs army post, Whitney had been missing in action. The young soldier had been found and cared for by villager women and brought to Mike's MASH unit. Whitney was now making progress, although she was still lapsing in and out of consciousness. She lay motionless, at her side was her husband.

He turned and stood from his chair at the sound of her footsteps. "Miss Alpert? It's good to see you in person."

"Please, call me Sarah. I can't tell you how wonderful it is to see you alive and well." Sarah's gaze fell to the unconscious young woman in the hospital bed. "I pray for her every day, John."

"Thank you. We need all the prayers we can get." He was too young to have so much worry on his face. "Her prognosis is good, although she is struggling. I can't tell you how much she enjoyed the card and letters your class sent us when we were serving overseas."

"I'm glad. The kids and I have missed being able to write to you two. When you both disappeared—" Emotion jammed into her windpipe, and she couldn't say the words. How many times had she feared the same would happen to Mike? She set her flowers down on the windowsill, squeezing it in between all the other bouquets. "I don't know all what you went through, but our prayers were with you then and are with you now. You should know the kids and I care."

"That means a lot." He was a sincere young man, handsome and likeable. A courageous soldier who had sacrificed a lot for this country. "One day soon Whitney is going to be able to come tell y'all herself."

"Any day now. As soon as Whitney is up to it, you two ought to come by. We will throw a cupcake party in your honor."

"It's a date." John's smile was strained. He looked as if he were tired and worried and struggling to hide it.

Her heart went out to him. She pulled a manila envelope out of her bag. "These are get-well notes and Christmas cards from the children. Is there anything at all I can do for you? I can sit here so you can grab a bite to eat? Fetch you a cup of tea? Run an errand for you?"

"That's nice of you, Sarah. Thank your class for me." He took the envelope, his eyes bright with emotion. "As for any errands, I'm good. All I need is right in this room."

"My cell number is on the card with the flowers. You call me if you need help with anything."

"I appreciate that."

"I plan on checking up on the two of you—" She paused, hearing a familiar child's voice down the hallway. It was Ali calling out for Dr. Mike.

Mike was here? Panic closed like a fist. She had to stay calm. She had to wrestle down the embarrassment busting to get out. She hoped what she managed was a polite goodbye. Her pulse thumped in her ears as she stepped out into the hall, turning toward him automatically.

He looked good. Powerful and confident as always in his white doctor's coat. His stethoscope hung around his neck. He held a chart in one hand. He hadn't noticed her yet, his attention was on Ali, who was chattering away a mile a minute. She couldn't seem to focus on what the boy was saying, but she was close enough now to see the dark circles beneath Mike's eyes. The hollows beneath his high cheekbones. The cut of strain on his chiseled face.

He didn't look as if he had been sleeping well. Something bad must have happened to him over there. She knew it. But what?

"Sarah!" Ali spotted her, running toward her with a note of anxiety. "I waited and waited."

"Everything is fine." She held out her hand, smiling reassuringly. "I was gone five minutes tops. Are you ready to head home?"

It was best to take the situation in hand. Let Mike know she hadn't been expecting to bump into him and now that she had, she would not be sticking around. He wouldn't need to worry about that. She set her chin, grappling down the memory of his rejection. He no longer loved her. She had ruined any chance of happiness long ago. She had to accept that. She had to learn to look him square in the eye. Just not yet.

"Come on, Ali. Mike, we'll get out of your way—"

"Sarah, you're not—"

"Good night." *Hold it together, Sarah.* She felt Ali's resistance, he didn't want to follow her down the hall, but she had to go. She had to get away from Mike because her eyes were stinging and her soul was cracking with grief.

Before, when he reenlisted against her wishes and got on that plane to the Middle East, she had been hurt and she had been mad, and those emotions had kept her from dealing with the absolute truth. Mike didn't love her. He didn't love her. There was nothing she could do to bring him back into her life. He was truly gone.

She jabbed the elevator button and willed the doors

to open. They didn't oblige. They remained staunchly closed, keeping her from escaping the knell of Mike's approaching footsteps.

Chapter Seven

"Wait a minute, Sarah. Don't go. Not like this." He hated that she was in such a hurry to escape him. Something was wrong, and he knew what. It wasn't easy, but he gathered up his courage and as she faced him, he fortified his defenses. He had to stay remote and unaffected. He had to approach this like the professional he was. "I didn't mean you had to avoid me."

She winced.

"I shouldn't have said some things to you." She glanced at the elevator doors looking like she wanted nothing more than to escape him. Her beautiful blue eyes pinched with pain. "Just a little embarrassed about that, to tell the truth."

Stay detached, he ordered himself. "You have nothing to be embarrassed about. It's forgotten."

"Oh." She looked down. Her shoulders slumped a little.

Too harsh, he realized. He hadn't meant to brush

aside her feelings. "I meant, we can leave that behind us. I don't want you to feel embarrassed about it."

"I see." That didn't help, either.

Maybe a little, he decided. He no longer knew. He had had a tough night and an even tougher day. "I'm pulling a double shift, so you'll have to forgive me."

"You're short staffed?"

"We're having more deployments, and you know what that's like. Folks have so much to get done before they head off for a year."

She nodded.

"Dr. Mike!" Ali hopped in place, all healthy little boy energy. Good to see.

"What is it—" *buddy,* he was going to say, but that wasn't right and it wasn't fair. It was going to be tough for them both but for the best in the long run. The pain was back, throbbing like a wound.

"I forgot to tell you somethin'." Ali grinned. "I colored a picture for you."

Stay impassive, Doctor, he commanded himself. "Nice."

"I don't got it with me. Soooo…" Ali drew out the word. "When can you come see it?"

He jammed his fists into his pockets. "I can't. I'm real busy here."

"Okay. Then how about tomorrow?" Hope filled those sweet brown eyes, full of innocence and trust.

"No." It was the toughest thing he had ever had to do. "I can't come."

"Then the next tomorrow?" That hope flickered, fragile and pure.

"No. I'm sorry, Ali. I promise to see you before Christmas." Christmas. There was a thought he couldn't stand. When times were tough during his deployment, he had planned a lot of things for his future. Ali's first American Christmas had been one of them.

"Ooookay." The boy sighed, wrestling with disappointment.

Yep, I how know you feel, little guy. The pain exploded. Best put an end to this agony. "Goodbye."

"Bye." Big soulful eyes stared up at him.

He was letting the little boy down. It destroyed him. It wasn't right. It wasn't fair. It had to be done. There was no changing that. He was Sarah's little boy. The two of them would share Christmas together and all the good times that went with the holiday. The two of them would be a family, a real family.

He wasn't part of that. Never would be. So he tucked away his own disappointments and secured the emotional perimeter.

Be in control, soldier, he demanded as one set of elevator doors yawned open. He felt nothing, nothing at all as the woman he once loved and the child he did boarded the elevator.

He did an about face and marched away. If he was going to stay in control of his emotions, he had to keep going. He couldn't take glancing over his shoulder as the doors were closing and seeing the sadness on Ali's little face. Mike couldn't take knowing he was the reason why.

* * *

At least she survived her run-in with Mike. Sarah looked up from her work. Today's classwork papers were scattered across the dining-room table. Clarence lay curled on top of a back couch cushion snoozing. The TV was on for noise, tuned to a classic movie channel, and the living room was alight with a black-and-white glow from the screen.

Mike. He had looked exhausted. This last year had changed him. His deployment had obviously been a tough one. Had he had someone to turn to?

She stuck a gold star on Amanda Mayhew's alphabet worksheet and added a smiley face. *She* had been the one Mike had turned to during his previous tours of duty. He was a man who kept to himself, who held in his emotions and disappointments, and she knew the pressures he worked under. He was a gifted surgeon, and he gave everything he had to his patients. She knew. There had been a time when she had wanted that kind of commitment from him, too.

She felt shame over that now. Mike's sincerity and devotion had been one of the things she admired about him right from the start. His desire to save others, to serve others made him the right kind of man, in her opinion. She knew that desire could eat him alive, if he wasn't careful. He tried so hard. He cared more than most.

Lord, please watch over him tonight. Help him find peace. The prayer rose from her heart without premeditation or thought. She checked Josie Mayhew's paper, fixed a gold star in the right hand corner and drew a smiley face.

"Noooooo. Noooooo." Ali's tortured cry echoed down the hall.

Sarah was on her feet, rushing toward his room. Not another nightmare. Poor baby. She padded into his room. Was he still asleep? "Ali?"

"Sarah!" He flew into her arms, sobs shaking him.

She felt hot tears against her throat as she lifted him into her lap. "It's all right. You're okay."

"Okay," he said through a sob. "My mama's all gone."

"I know. I'm sorry." She kissed the crown of his head, blinking hard.

Olga Terenkov, the grief counselor at the church, had assured her these nightmares were perfectly normal. There were so many emotions and anxieties children Ali's age didn't know how to verbalize.

"I dreamed that I l-lost her." Ali's voice went high and thin. "We was in a market and I looked and looked for her."

"She's in Heaven watching over you."

"That's what the pastor says."

Pastor Fields. Sarah snuggled her boy a little tighter. "Our minister is very smart. I'm sure he's right."

Ali fell silent, breathing hard as he wrestled down his sobs. She started to hum a comforting tune, one her mother had sang to her when she was little. The child in her arms began to relax.

"S-Sarah?"

She leaned her cheek against his soft hair. "What is it, honey?"

"You won't leave, will you?"

"No. I'll be right here. I'll always be here for you."

"Okay." Ali sighed, his arms wrapping tighter around her neck. "I think my mama would like that."

Her eyes burned. The tears she had been holding back slipped down her face. She prayed for the woman she had never known half a world away who had been killed senselessly. She prayed for this child and for the children everywhere who were hurting. She prayed for the soldiers who risked their lives to protect all of them. Hours passed and still she held Ali, hoping her love was enough to keep his nightmares at bay.

The ground quaked beneath his feet hard enough to jar him and rock the monitors. Good thing he had braced himself. The overhead lights dimmed and brightened. The mortar strike had been close. Too close. Again.

"At least there aren't any bullets this time." Judging by his tone, Tom was grinning behind his mask. "It's kind of funny how you get used to this."

"You ain't seen nothing yet." The real concern was getting this bleeding stopped. Liver wounds were tricky. "I'm not losing this kid. Carrie, how's his pressure?"

"Steady for now."

That hadn't always been the case. His patient—Ben Sutton—was just twenty-one years old. Mike thought of his mother somewhere stateside who might not yet know he was gravely injured, Ben had been choppered off the battlefield. He thought of all the people back home who loved and cared about this boy. He thought of the long, good life Ben deserved.

You can't let him die, Montgomery. The back of his neck burned from what was already a long night of work. The kid's liver was a mess. "We've got to excise this half here. There's no saving it. Then maybe he's got a chance. Tom, grab—"

"Doctor, he's dropping. Fast."

The monitor flatlined. Just like that. "Don't you die on me, Ben. C'mon—" But he stood helpless as his team burst to life around him. He was frozen in time, unable to move, unable to make a difference.

You have to save Ben, he scolded himself. *Do something. Anything—*

Mike shot awake, sitting up in the dark. Where was he? His harsh, rasping breathing echoed in the stillness. Sweat poured off him. His hands were shaking. He'd had the dream again, the one where he'd stood motionless, dreaming that he was unable to help, suspended in time.

That wasn't how it happened, but the dream kept haunting him. Failure, dark and deep, grasped his soul. He hung his head and tried to still his breathing. He was home now. Gone were the blood-soaked scrubs and young Ben Sutton lifeless on his table. What lingered was the suffocating sense of failure.

I did everything right. He pressed his hands to his face. *I did everything there was to do.*

But it hadn't been enough. He hadn't been enough.

He had fought for Ben's life as if it were his own. No one could have done more. His team had reassured him of that. His commanding officer had confirmed it. Losing a soldier on his table made a piece of him die, too. There had been too many losses on this last deployment; too much of him was missing.

How did he get the image of Ben Sutton out of his mind? Mike rubbed his eyes, threw back the twisted sheets and climbed out of bed. He didn't know what he needed. He didn't know what would help.

Just keep walking, Major. He wandered down the dark hall into the kitchen. The ambient light from the microwave and stove clock cast enough glow for him to get a glass of water without turning on the lights. He didn't want lights. He felt if he stayed hidden in the shadows, his failures would have a harder time of finding him. He knew it wasn't true, but it helped him to get through the night.

He chugged down the fresh, cool water and tried to swallow another thought as well. There was another glaring reason he wasn't doing so well this time out. He had an overwhelming need to pick up the phone and dial her number. Hearing Sarah's voice and her gentle understanding could always soothe him.

He squeezed his eyes shut, set the glass on the counter and willed his mind to stop. He couldn't allow himself to even think about reaching out to her. He was alone now. He had to deal. He had to stand on his own feet. It didn't pay to lean on other people.

In the end, you were alone anyway.

Alone, he headed down the hall, knowing he didn't have a chance in heaven to get back to sleep. Dawn wasn't far away.

Saturday morning came too soon. Sarah had managed to grab some sleep on the other twin bed in Ali's room and the rest of his night had gone smoothly, but she had kept waking up to check on him. She felt as if she were stumbling around the kitchen finishing up the breakfast dishes.

She had made Ali's favorite breakfast of pancakes with a smiling strawberry jam mouth, two blueberries for eyes and chocolate syrup for hair. He'd been hungry and with his second stack, he made his own faces with the strips of bacon and chocolate chips. Not the most nutritious breakfast on earth, but at least he was smiling. His losses weren't forgotten, but at least they weren't weighing on him.

"Clarence loves me." Ali sat in the middle of the living room floor with the cat on his lap, squeezing him with both arms. The cat lay limp, enduring the public display of affection. "I love him, too. He's my friend."

"Yes, he is." Sarah rinsed the last of the silverware and dumped it into the dishwasher basket. "Only a true friend would let you hug him like that."

"You know what?"

Uh-oh. She recognized that mischievous look in those sweet brown eyes. "What?"

"Dr. Mike's my friend."

Oh, boy, here we go again. She pushed the bottom rack in and closed the dishwasher door. "Mike is very much your friend, but you and I have another busy day."

"'Cuz we're seein' Dr. Mike?" Ali gave Clarence a final squeeze and released him.

"Mike probably has a thousand things to do. He got back from deployment a week ago. Besides, the two of us have plans."

"We do?"

As if she hadn't told him yesterday. Thinking about seeing Mike used to have that effect on her, too, it made everything else unimportant. "We have the little matter of doing our shopping and picking out our Christmas tree."

"We're gonna put it here." Ali skipped over to where one couch stood in front of the front window. He spread his arms wide, indicating the exact spot.

"That's a good spot." After she shoved the couch to the other side of the room, of course. "We can keep the blinds up at night so everyone going by can see the Christmas-tree lights, too."

"That's what Dr. Mike said."

Somehow she was going to have to get used to the stabbing pains in her chest at the mention of Mike's name. Ali was not going to stop talking about his hero any time soon. She had to learn to cope.

She grabbed the hand towel from the oven handle. "Turn the TV off for me, please. We've got to get started on our errands."

"Okay." Ali seemed particularly eager. He hopped over to the remote, hit it and dropped it back on the coffee table on his way through the room. He was moving at a good clip. He must be really excited about getting a tree.

Good. She wanted to make the day as easy as possible for him. Clarence wrapped around her ankles on his way to his water bowl. She ran her fingertips through his soft fur and was rewarded with a rusty purr. She made sure he had some dry food to snack on in his food dish before she gathered up her purse and keys.

Ali breezed into sight with a grin on his face. He had changed into the T-shirt and matching sweatshirt that Mike had sent him several months ago.

"You look handsome. Are you ready to go?"

"Yep." He stood military straight in front of her, except for that adorable, wide grin, the cutie.

She loved this little boy. Although she wasn't his adopted mom yet, it sure felt as if she was as she handed him his coat and hat and helped him into both. She thought about the life she had dreamed about with Mike and the future she had expected to have with him.

It was strange how life had a way of working out. He was right. That dream hadn't been meant for them, but she was beginning to see the wisdom behind God's plan for her. It might have been hard on her heart losing Mike, but look at what she had gained. A life she wasn't constantly chasing after trying to catch hold of. She had a sweet little boy to love. She had a family.

Who knew where God's path would take her next? Wherever it was, it would be good. For the first time in a long while, she believed without doubt. Her faith may be new, but it was strengthening by the day.

While she locked up, Ali knelt down to look at the rocks in the flowerbed. Finding none, he took her hand.

As they walked the short distance to the carport in the back, they had a perfect view of Marlon's house, Ali's grandfather who had passed away recently. The house sat dark and closed up. A flash of red and white caught her attention.

A realtor sign. The house was up for sale. Somehow that made his passing even sadder. Soon the home would sell and new people would move in, as if to erase the memory of the terse curmudgeon who had lived there. Marlon was all bark and no bite, she had learned. She had cared for him. Underneath his gruffness, he had been a good man.

Ali didn't notice the sign. He was staring straight up at the sky, watching for helicopters flying on training missions from the post.

"Sarah?"

"What is it?"

"We're gonna get a big tree, right?"

"A *big* tree, sure. Just not a *gigantic* tree because it won't fit in the living room."

That made him giggle. He clapped his hands together bounding up to the SUV. "Okay, a big tree!"

"Think of all the lights we can put on it." Sarah unlocked his door.

"A hundred." Ali climbed into the backseat. His shadowed eyes hinted at his tough night, but his smile was bright and full of promise. "A hundred hundred! A zillion."

"I don't know. A zillion is an awful lot of lights." Sarah couldn't help joking as she helped him with his car seat buckle. "I know I don't have that many lights in storage. We'll have to buy more."

"Lots more. Flashing ones." He grinned, all buckled up.

She laughed, shutting the back door. "Oh, no. Not more flashing lights."

"Yep! They're the best."

"I don't know about that." She kept her voice light, so he would know she was joking with him. As she slid behind the wheel, she saw his cute button face in her rearview mirror and her heart squeezed with an ever-deeper love. "I was planning on white lights. The kind that don't flash at all."

"Sarah!" Ali shook his head. "Don't you know the flashing ones are better?"

"I suppose you're right," she agreed, starting the engine. "But if we want a zillion lights, we are going to have to put buying them on our errand list."

"Okay." Ali sounded so eager. He clapped his hands again.

She remembered being five and going with her parents and older sister to get their tree. She backed out of the driveway into the street. "You can pick out your ornaments, too."

"I want soldiers like Dr. Mike."

How did she know? Sarah tried not to roll her eyes as she drove down the street. A military theme would be an interesting complement to her precious porcelain ornaments she had collected over the years. Ornaments, she realized with a start, that were ones Mike had given her. While her mother had started the collection long ago for her, Sarah added to it yearly. And when she and Mike had become serious, he had always bought her one as a surprise during the Christmas season.

Well, maybe she would keep those wrapped up in their storage boxes another year. She would see how many boxes of glass ball ornaments she could fit into her budget. The fewer reminders of Mike the better.

"Wait. This isn't the way to Dr. Mike's!" Ali's cheer was gone.

When she checked the mirror, she saw him swiveling around, looking around. Gone, too, was his calm. Distressed, he struggled against his seat belt.

"Sarah, you go the wrong way." Emotion thinned his voice. He sounded so small and vulnerable. "We got to get Dr. Mike."

Mike? Where had he gotten such an idea? Sarah checked for traffic and pulled over to the curb. "Honey, Mike is busy doing his own stuff. Why are you crying? Here, let me get a tissue."

"He's supposed to come with us."

"Did he tell you so?" She remembered the night when she had been visiting with John in Whitney's room. Ali and Mike had been alone chatting for a bit. Maybe they had discussed it then? It was the only thing that made sense.

"Yes. He said—" He hiccoughed. "When we was puttin' up the lights—"

"On the house?"

"Yes. He said we was gonna put the tree at the window. He s-said it. He did."

"Okay. It's all right." She wedged herself between the front seats to gently wipe away his tears. She couldn't imagine Mike making that promise, so it only stood to reason Ali had misunderstood. It wouldn't be the first time. He wanted to spend time with Mike so badly, was all. She hated the heartbreak on his face. He needed Mike. It was that simple.

I need your help to ease out of his life. He's more dependent than I thought. Mike's words came back to her. Typical Mike. Relationships were easy for him, simple, black and white. She had always been the one trying so hard, she could see that now. She could recognize it easier looking at Ali, all tears and heartbreak. He had grown to love the man who had stepped into a protective father role when Ali had been alone in a wartorn part of the world, and now Mike just thought he could waltz away. No harm, no foul.

Well, she had a thing or two to say to the man. She had always kept her cool. She was the one who tried hard to see the other side of every argument most of the time. But not now. She grabbed her cell and made a call.

"You just forgot, right, Sarah?" Ali sniffled. "You gonna turn around now so we can see Dr. Mike?"

"Don't you worry. I'll take care of it." She waited for the phone to connect, her heart pounding. No answer. So she pounded out a text message. *Town center at eleven o'clock. Ali needs you. Don't be late.*

She didn't add that he had better be there. Mike Montgomery was a good man in countless ways, but she was not going to let him get away with making her little boy cry. Mike Montgomery had finally met his match, and the poor man had no idea.

She tucked her phone back into her purse, made sure Ali was snug and safe and pulled back out into traffic. It was 9:35 in the morning and already it felt like a very long day.

Chapter Eight

Mike checked his watch. It was exactly eleven hundred. Where was she? The streets were jammed today. Everyone had errands of their own, and he was no exception. He had ditched his to-do list halfway through just to be here as Sarah asked. As his watch ticked off another minute, he scanned the Christmas-tree lot and the carolers standing on the front steps of the church.

Wait a minute, he sure hoped this had nothing to do with church. Sarah had been trying to get him to join before their breakup.

"Dr. Mike!" Ali's call across the street noise had him turning around. Relief washed over him. From Sarah's abrupt message, he had thought something was really wrong. But the kid looked great as he ran a half a step ahead of Sarah, dragging her with him.

"You came!" Ali skidded to a stop.

It was the doctor in him that had him checking Ali's respiration rate—fast, but then he had been running.

Studying his color. Noticing the red rimmed eyes. "Sure I came. Are you okay?"

Ali nodded. "'Cuz you're here."

Uh-oh. Mike kept his gaze down, fixed firmly on the child so he didn't have to look at the woman. But her suede boots came into view and he didn't have to look up to know she was angry with him. He could feel it like the cold in the wind.

"What's going on?" He had to ask; he had no idea.

"You and Ali are going to pick out a Christmas tree together." Sarah's tone was no nonsense and firm, her teacher's voice. She meant business. "You are going to pick out the biggest tree that will fit in my living room."

"I am?" That was news to him.

"Yep, like you said." Ali took his hand and held on so tight.

Mike, braced against it, could feel that need. It was like the surface temperature of the sun. "I never said."

"You did." Ali, all sincerity, began looking worried. "Right? You're gonna stay with me?"

Bull's-eye. That was like a bullet to the heart. How was he going to say no to that? Now he was beginning to understand why she was mad at him. "Sarah, I never said. I'll do what he needs, but just so you know—"

"Oh, I know."

Mad wasn't the word. Smoldering mad would be a better description. Sarah was quiet even when she was furious. He had better brace himself.

"You, Michael Adam Montgomery, had better watch

what you say to him." Her eyes sparked blue fire. "English is not his first language. He thinks you said you would pick out a Christmas tree with him, and that is exactly what you are going to do. Do you understand, Major?"

"Yes, ma'am." He was a smart enough man to know when he was licked. And more important was the little boy clinging to him. Sarah was right. Ali's need was more significant than Mike had figured. He had things to do, but they could wait.

"I understand."

"And make sure the tree isn't too tall." She reached into her tidy shoulder bag and handed him a fold of twenties. "This should be enough—"

"No, I don't feel right taking your money."

"I won't have you buying my tree."

Ouch. Gone was the hurting woman asking for his forgiveness. Worse, he understood what she meant. They were no longer in love. They were no longer friends. It was best to be clear about that. He took the money, but he didn't like it. "Do I get to keep the change?"

The corners of her mouth twitched. "No. I'll expect a receipt, too. I don't trust you."

He had almost made her smile. "Yes, ma'am. What do you think, Ali? Think we can find the best tree?"

"We can! Know what, Dr. Mike?"

"I'm not your doctor anymore. Maybe you had better start calling me Mike. Just plain Mike."

"Mike." Ali gave it a try and grinned. "Do you know what, Mike?"

"I'm afraid to ask what."

"I'm wearing the shirt." The kid patted his chest, where his shirt showed through his partially zipped jacket. "It's like yours."

"It is." Beneath his jacket, Mike also wore a gray shirt with U.S. Army printed across the front in bold letters.

"We match like socks." Ali laughed.

That was one of Sarah's sayings. Cute, but the truth was, she read too many children's books. Her life was fairy-tale worlds with puppy-dog endings. He supposed he always resented that, maybe even looked down on it a little. It wasn't the world he knew existed.

But he had never wanted anything more. He clamped his mouth shut, just in case momentary weakness took him over. He was not going to reminisce. He wasn't going to long for a long-ago sweetness.

"You have an hour to find a tree." She pushed up her coat sleeve to check her watch.

"Got it." He studied her for a moment. "I'll take Ali to lunch, and then we'll report home around one o'clock. I'll get the tree inside for you and be on my way. How does that sound?"

"Fine." Since there was nothing more to say, Sarah took a step back. "Ali, you have fun with Mike. I'll see you soon."

"But you need to come."

"You and Mike will have a fun time together. Isn't that what you wanted?"

Ali nodded, then shook his head.

She knew what the boy wanted. He needed as much

adult security and care as he could get. He needed to know he wasn't alone in the world, after losing his entire family. He also needed to know that wherever he went or whatever happened, she was going to be waiting for him. "Guess what I want you to do?"

"What?" Curious, Ali leaned close, eyes wide.

"I want you to have the best time ever with Mike." She knelt down and brushed dark brown hair from his eyes. "You find the best tree. And when you come home, I want you to tell me all about it."

"Everything?"

"Everything." She kissed his cheek. "Have fun. I'll see you at thirteen hundred hours."

"How many is that?"

"Ask Mike." It wasn't easy to stand. Her knees were wobbly. She wanted to believe it was the after effects of her little bout of temper, but she knew better. It was Mike. She wasn't immune to him. She would never be immune to him. Her heart had a mind of its own, and there was nothing she could do to stop loving him.

So the wisest course was to simply walk away and keep walking.

"I want this one!" Ali tilted his head all the way back to see to the very top of the giant spruce. He flung his arms wide. "It's really big, Dr. Mike! I mean, Mike."

What was he going to do with the kid? Mike shook his head. "That looks to be the biggest one in the whole lot. Trouble is, it won't fit in Sarah's living room."

"Are you sure?"

"Positive." He bit his tongue to keep from adding *buddy*. Whatever happened, this was nothing more than a rescue mission. He had come because the boy had been upset. He was the kind of man who did the right thing. This excursion with Ali was nothing more than a step away from the friends they used to be. He didn't like it, not one bit, but that was the way life was sometimes. "Let's look for something a little smaller."

"Yep." Ali blew out a breath of air, scrunching up his face, button-cute. The little guy tromped to the next grouping of trees, bright with wonder, as he studied each fir and spruce and pine imagining which would be his perfect Christmas tree.

"Not these two," Mike pointed out, gesturing toward a pair of the Douglas firs. "Too tall."

"How about this one?" Ali tugged on a lower branch of a spruce. "It's almost as tall and it's real soft. It's got lots of arms."

"Branches—" *buddy*. He bit off the word. "Let's keep this one in mind and keep looking."

"Someone else might get it." A line of worry crinkled his forehead.

"I'll take care of it." Mike grabbed a sold tag from the kiosk and told the fellow there, "We're still looking."

"I get that all the time." The older man winked. "You and your son take all the time looking you want."

Your son.

"Thanks." Not bothering to correct the man, he trailed after the little boy who darted from tree to tree. Protective urges roared to the surface.

What he felt was more than wanting to protect and provide for the boy. It was a soul-deep commitment to Ali's life.

"Look at this, Mike!" The boy danced with excitement in front of a tall slender tree.

"I s-see." The word stuck in his throat. He had to get his emotions under control.

"It's not as good," Ali decided after serious contemplation. "It's too short and it's pointy."

"It's a ponderosa pine. Their needles are stiffer." Clinical, that was the way to handle this. "What else do you see?"

"Hmm." Ali wandered off, staring up at the tops of the trees. "Is that one too tall?"

"You know it." Mike winked. "We would have to cut a hole through Sarah's attic and roof to get that tree to stand upright."

Ali laughed, a happy, carefree sound. It was a tribute to Sarah and her loving heart that Ali was doing as well as he was. That he could set aside the hardships of his earlier life long enough to dance through a tree lot, imagining twinkle lights and Christmas angels hanging from branches.

What he couldn't let himself admit was that he missed Sarah and her loving heart, too. He swallowed hard against a lump of emotion rising in his windpipe. Best not to feel that, either. Boy, she had been mad at him. He caught himself smiling as he followed Ali to the far edge of the tree lot. He could still see her standing in front of him, her temper flaring. It was a rare occurrence, but she was never lovelier than when she was putting him in his place.

"Do you still like the first one?" he asked the kid.

"Yep. That's the bestest."

"Then let's buy it, get it loaded and stop for some pizza. What do you think of that plan?"

"It's a good one 'cuz I'm hungry." Ali's grin could tempt a man to want to love and protect the little guy even more.

Another wave of mortification washed over her when she spotted Mike hiking up her walkway hefting an eight-foot fir. She heard Ali fumbling with the knob and had just enough time to grab the bags of unwrapped presents and squirrel them away into the pantry closet before the front door swung wide and in came a clapping Ali.

"Look, Sarah. We got us the tallest one that we didn't have to cut a hole for."

That sounded like Mike's sense of humor. She rescued Clarence, who was looking alarmed, from the back of the couch and cradled him. Branches rustled, Mike's breathing rasped and then the tree whisked into the house.

"Right here!" Ali hopped up and down in front of the space she had cleared. He sure looked like one happy boy. Judging by the looks of things, he had a good time.

Calling Mike had been the right thing to do. Knowing that made some of the tightness in her stomach ease, but not all of it. She had been so angry with him. She still was, as a matter of fact. Keeping his back to her as he worked the tree into the stand she had left out right in front of the window, acting as if everything was just peachy. It wasn't. Not even close.

Fortunately for him, the phone rang. Since he and Ali were busy, she carried Clarence with her and caught it on the second ring. "Hello?"

"Sarah, glad I found you in." It was Olga from the church grief center and her bubbly voice was like spring in full blossom. "I'm sorry I haven't been able to get back to you sooner. Everything is crazy here. So much to do! How is Ali?"

"Right now he is running in circles around our Christmas tree. We just put it up."

"Excellent." Olga's laugh was contagious and caring, as if she could just picture how cute that really was.

Sarah had a hard time keeping hold of her anger. Mike had stepped back to survey his work while Ali zipped faster and faster, his sneakers beating a loud rhythm. Clarence apparently had enough of the noise and wanted down, so Sarah let him onto the counter. He flicked his tail, perhaps at Mike's presence, and leaped onto the top of the refrigerator, one of his favorite spots.

She stepped into the kitchen, so Mike wouldn't overhear. "He's a little fragile today, but doing well. He had another tough night."

"Nightmares, poor boy." Olga sympathized. She was a woman who understood grief, having lost her husband in the Soviet war in Afghanistan nearly twenty years ago. "Do you want to bring him in this afternoon?"

"I was hoping that we could talk."

"Absolutely. You name the time and I'll come over for a visit. That way Ali can stay and play where he's secure and you and I can have a heart to heart."

"I would love that, Olga." She needed guidance on all fronts. Prayer, she knew, would help, and so would Olga's experience. "I'll make a pot of tea and some brownies."

"Oh, brownies. The magic word. You will be sorry when you can't get rid of me. Or at least until every crumb is gone."

Sarah laughed, relieved she was not alone. It wasn't as if she could turn to Mike. "Please come anytime that's good for you."

"In an hour or so. You need time to bake. I have a good feeling about our talk. Don't think I haven't forgotten you said no to my last singles activity." Olga also managed the church's single's events. "We're having another session of matchmaking trivia night this week right before our singles Christmas party. Should I expect you?"

"I'm sorry. That's the night of our school concert."

"There's always next time!" Olga hung up laughing.

A singles party. Sarah hung up, knowing it was going to be hard to get out of going eventually. But the sight of Mike standing in her living room made her reconsider. Since they had left the door wide open, she walked over to quietly close it. Somehow she was going to have to get used to the idea of dating again. Someday.

"Sarah!" Ali, tiring of his laps around the tree, stopped to drag in a dramatic breath. It was good to see him so happy and active. "The lights, please. So Mike and me, we can put 'em up. Like outside."

Uh-oh. Sarah turned to Mike and their gazes connected. Longing jolted through her, unwanted and unbidden. When was this going to stop?

Mike cleared his throat. "Sorry, Ali. I don't think that's what Sarah had in mind. This is your first Christmas with her. You two should do the decorating together."

"It's my Christmas with you, too." Confusion crinkled across his forehead. Wide, honest eyes stared up at her. "Sarah, Mike's gotta stay, right?"

"Mike has his own things to do." She prayed that she sounded sure and calm and her heart was safely tucked away. "The two of us can put up our new ornaments together. Won't that be fun?"

"But what about Mike?" Ali looked anxiously to his champion. "He's gotta stay, too!"

"No, kid. It's time for me to go." Mike yanked the boy's hat off by the ball on top. "But will you do something for me?"

Ali nodded gravely, grabbing on to Mike with both hands.

"You have to take care of Sarah. Make sure she has a good time getting the tree just right." Mike dropped the hat on the arm of the nearby couch and knelt to help Ali out of his coat. "It's an important job. Think you can do it for me?"

"N-no. Y-yes." Ali's bottom lip trembled. "Don't leave, Mike. Don't go."

"I've got to. This isn't my tree. This isn't my house." *And you're not my son.* Mike bit back those words and the surprising bitterness with them.

If anyone besides Sarah had started adoption proce-
dures, he would be in there, fighting tooth and nail. He
wished he could do that to Sarah, but he couldn't. He
stood instead, doing what was right, doing what had to
be done. Excising every last bit of his heart, he strode
past her to the door. He didn't look at her. He didn't
think he had the strength to. Having him around was
hurting her as surely as it was hurting him. There was
only one thing to do. Ali didn't really need him. He had
everything he needed here with Sarah.

"I'll call you next week, Ali." He stopped on the top
step. Something held him back. He hated to think it was
emotions he had no right feeling. "Tell you what. You
can come help me pick out and decorate my tree."

Instead of being glad at the prospect, Ali's eyes filled.
Why? The little guy stood there, fists clenched at his
sides, his mouth in a downturn and tears rolling silently
down his cheeks, then he stormed out to this bedroom.
Mike felt helpless. He'd thought the boy had loved
going to the tree lot.

"You." Sarah came at him like a four-star general.
"That's twice now you have made him cry, and I won't
have it. You can't treat him like that."

"Like what?" He felt as if his chest was being
cracked open. "I'm doing what's right. Are you going
to tell me that you want me to stick around?"

"What I want you to do is not to treat him the way
you do the rest of us. Making him care. Making him
promises. He expects you are going to be here for him,
but you're doing what you always do. You're keeping

him at arm's length and acting as if you don't have a clue when it breaks his heart."

"Whoa, there." He held up both hands. "That's not what I do, Sarah. You're the one adopting him. Not me."

That stopped her. There were tears in her eyes, too, shimmering and vulnerable. "I can't say that I want you here. I wanted to pick the tree out with Ali. I want to decorate it with him, just the two of us. But look at him."

"I see." Ali had pressed his face to the front window, tears rolling down his face, so little and vulnerable. "I didn't think he would react like this."

"Me, either. He's more attached to you than either of us realized." Sarah turned away, shaking her head, scattering the fall of her red hair that gleamed like a dream as she went back inside the house to comfort her foster son.

Mike's throat went scratchy. He didn't mean to pry, but he couldn't seem to look away. The picture she made as she went down on both knees to pull the boy into her arms was something he had envisioned more than a few times. Once, when he pictured his future, he had always seen Sarah and their child, just like that.

All he knew, was that he could no longer walk away. Not like this. He was at a loss. He had thought Ali wouldn't mind so much, it was simply the matter of spending less time with him until the boy didn't notice he was gone. After all, he had a busy, happy life with Sarah. Why would Ali want him, too?

He hated it when he was wrong. So he ambled back into the house and shut the door.

"I'm going to make some brownies," Sarah was saying as she wiped away the last of Ali's tears and stood. "We'll put off decorating the tree for a while. Mike, do you want to stay?"

"I've got to." He drew himself up straight. The fortifications around his heart were more important than ever. He held out his hand. "C'mon, Ali. Let's put our feet up and see if there's a game on."

"Okay." With a sniffle, the boy came to him. He wrapped his fingers around Mike's so tight, he was bound to cut off circulation. "Good." Ali let out a shaky breath, as if his anxieties were abating.

"I'll be in the kitchen." Sarah came close enough to gently ruffle the boy's hair, all affection and sweetness.

She took the last whole piece of him as she walked away. Mike closed his eyes, lost and wishing he could find his way.

It was starting to be too much.

Chapter Nine

"Don't forget Wednesday night, seven-thirty. Match-making trivia night." Olga gathered up her purse and bag and the package of brownies. "Say, Mike? You can come, too. Even if you aren't a member, we would love to have a handsome, strapping doctor like you."

"I'm working, I think. Or on call. I can't remember, but I'm sure it's one of those."

"Excuses, excuses. There are two things a man can't hide from forever, Mike Montgomery, God and true love." Olga had a way about her that was both strong and inviting, and she flashed Sarah a private wink. "It's the tall, strong silent types that get my heart every time. I'm sure you know exactly what I mean."

Did she. Although was she going to admit it? No. Sarah opened the door for her friend. "I'm assuming you are talking about Pastor Fields?"

"Franklin." Olga sighed, her affections for the minister no secret to anyone. "That man sees me and thinks, oh, there's the woman who makes those great homemade pierogies. We had the worst first date in recorded history. Not, oh, there goes the love of my life."

"Maybe that's what he's thinking secretly." Sarah couldn't think of a better match than Olga with their dear pastor.

"He needs time, or so I hear." Olga stepped out into the cold night. Maybe it was the darkness, but the vivacious woman looked uncharacteristically bleak. "I fear it's a kind excuse because he doesn't want to hurt my feelings."

"I'm praying for you, Olga. You deserve a good man like Pastor Fields."

"Bless you. Now, enough of my woes. You think on what I've said, and I'll check with you tomorrow after church. We will get this worked out for Ali, you'll see."

"Thank you, Olga." She believed in this woman. Already she had done so much for Ali. "Drive safely."

"Will do. Have a lovely evening!" Olga tapped down the sidewalk to her car parked at the curb.

Sarah waited a moment to make sure her friend was in her car and on her way, before she closed the door and turned to the boys on her couch. They were taking in the highlights on one of the sports channels. Now, that was a sound she had surprisingly missed. It reminded her of all the cozy winter afternoons they had spent together, Mike watching a game while she sat reading or working on lesson plans.

"I'm not going to any singles event, especially at a church." Mike watched her over the back of the couch.

Maybe a smile was hovering in the corners of his stern mouth. "I hope you're not going to get mad at me about that."

Oh, so he *was* joking. "Then you just be careful not to cross me, or you might just have to."

He arched one brow, as if he were trying to figure out if she was serious or joking right along with him. Well, let him wonder. She had enough on her hands trying not to see both the past and the future she had lost. "Olga has helped Ali tremendously."

"She's nice," Ali added, hopping up onto his knees on the cushions. He propped his elbows on the back of the couch and rested his chin in his hands. "Sarah, do you know what?"

"I'm afraid to ask, cutie."

"Mike's gonna see me tomorrow."

"Is that right?" Mike had turned toward her, and she could feel his intense scrutiny. Typical Mike, she couldn't begin to guess at his emotions from his stony expression, but Ali's wide grin had to be a clue. "What are you two boys up to?"

"Boy stuff."

"What exactly is that?"

Ali shrugged. "I dunno. But I get to see Mike."

"That's right, Ali." Mike reached for the remote and clicked off the TV. "We're going to play a little basketball, like last week—"

"And Sarah can come with us, too, some?"

"You didn't let me finish." Mike was gentle, but firm. "But we're going to do some things different, too. It's just going to be you and me and maybe we might get ice cream instead of pizza."

"Ice cream for dinner?" Ali shook his head. "That's not right. Sarah says it has to be a food goop."

"Food group," she quickly corrected. "I'm going to leave you boys to finish making your plans. I've got dinner to get started on."

"Can Mike stay?"

Before she could answer, Mike was already shaking his head. "Sorry. But do you know what? If you get to missing me, you can call me. How about that?"

"Okay. I can call you now?"

"If you want to."

"Can I call you in an hour?"

"Yep. I'll even answer."

"How about in two hours?"

Sarah took her escape, trying to hold back the rising swell of gratitude. She wanted to stay angry at him. Anger was easier. Anger gave her a reason to push him away. It made her forget how very much she loved the man.

Clarence slitted open his eyes and watched her from the top of the fridge. She pulled a can of stewed tomatoes from the pantry shelf and heard a familiar step behind her.

Mike. He stood in the archway, one wide shoulder against the wall. "Is that what I did to you? Did I keep you at arm's length?"

"You know you did." She set the can on the counter. Did Mike really look bewildered? Did he really not have a clue? "All I wanted was to be closer to you. All through college, it was your studies in the way. Then when you were in medical school, you hardly had any time for me."

"Sarah, I couldn't help that. I thought you understood—"

"I did. You wanted to become a doctor, and I wanted that for you. So I waited for you. All those nights you were on duty, I went to bed without a call from you. Those days when you were making rounds and taking classes, I went without seeing you. With every deployment, I was right here carrying my cell everywhere in case you had time to call. I loved you enough to wait."

He didn't move. He probably didn't even get what she was trying to say. It didn't matter anyway. They were over. She knelt down to pull a deep-sided skillet from the cabinet. "You were always promising, and I was always waiting. It wasn't until today that I realized the truth. That with you, I would have always been waiting. This isn't about the army or you committing to me. It's that I was never the woman you were going to open your heart to."

"That's what you think?"

"It's what I know." Gently, she set the skillet on the burner, feeling stronger. Somehow she felt free, to say the words to him. "I'm sorry I was angry at you earlier."

"I deserved it. Are you still mad at me?"

"Not like I was. I was just as much to blame. It's taken this last year to see what love really is."

"You mean it's not all roses and wishes and wedding plans?"

"Now you're teasing me, Major. Love is many

things, but I hadn't realized it is mostly duty. So that said, I've got some cooking to do. Are you going to take off?"

"Yeah." He looked as if he was about to say something more but changed his mind. "I'll be by to pick up Ali after church. I will take care with him. He's what matters now. You and I have that in common."

"We do." She liked that Mike smiled at her. She was surprised how easy it was to smile in return. For the first time she felt peaceful in his presence. They were united in purpose, and it felt comfortable. Right. She couldn't see God's plan, but she trusted it.

"Good night, Mike."

"Take care, Sarah." She heard his footsteps retreat to the living room. His voice rumbled low, and Ali's sweet voice answered. They talked together before the door whispered open and clicked closed.

Ali's sneakers squeaked on the hardwood. "Sarah, do you know what?"

She pulled out the cutting board and a knife. "What?"

"Mike sure is nice."

"Uh-huh." She knew firsthand that Mike could be very nice. "You two had fun today. I know you miss him."

"Yeah. I miss lots of people." Ali ambled over to the refrigerator and raised his hand toward Clarence. He went up on tiptoe. Then he jumped. "I miss Grandpa. I miss my mom."

"I know you do." Sarah left the counter to crouch down so she could be on Ali's level. She waited for whatever it was he needed to say.

"Mike isn't going to go to Heaven, too?"

"Not that we know about."

Ali nodded and grabbed her hand hard. "When people go away, sometimes they go there."

"Sometimes, that's true, but I'm not going anywhere. Whatever happens you aren't going to be alone. I promise you that."

Ali looked so sad. "I don't like being all alone. I like being with you, Sarah. And Mike, too."

"I like being with you. Oh—" The phone rang, startling her. "Why don't we see who that is?"

"Is it Mike?"

"He just left, silly." Sarah chuckled, kissed his cheek and reached to grab the cordless. She recognized her mom's number on the screen. Not surprising, as she usually called every Saturday evening. "It's for you."

"Nanny Alice!" Ali grabbed the phone, eager to talk to his new grandmother. "Hello! Hello!"

Bless Mom, Sarah thought as she watched the boy dance around the kitchen. She and Dad had unconditionally accepted her decision to be a foster parent, and had been involved and loving first with Carlos and now Ali.

And bless Olga, she added. Ali was beginning to talk about his losses. That was a big step. But right now he was chattering on about the Christmas tree and how big it was and how he had helped Mike tie it to the top of the car.

I'm going to have to explain about Mike, Sarah reminded herself as she opened the refrigerator door and earned a scowl from Clarence.

* * *

Mike had a lot on his mind as he pulled into his assigned parking space and killed the engine. He found himself staring up at the lights of the medical center, blazing like a beacon of hope against the coming darkness. Sunset stained the underbellies of clouds and streaked the fading blue of the Texas sky. He'd meant to head home, but didn't want to face the emptiness his life had become.

Maybe it just seemed empty, he told himself as he locked up and hiked across the lot. Being with Ali today had been like getting back a tiny piece of himself. Sitting on Sarah's couch like old times with her baking brownies in the kitchen and chatting with her had been a balm to the restless loneliness that haunted him.

It wasn't like he wanted her back or anything. But her accusation had stirred him up some. He didn't intentionally keep people at a distance. She had it all turned around. She really did. He had let her closer than anyone. She had been family to him; the woman he intended to marry. He'd been committed to her heart and soul, as much as he had of either to give anyhow.

No, he thought as he missed a step. She wasn't right. She was hurt and angry, that's why she said those things. She had been emotional over Ali. That's all.

"Major." He was saluted by Jim, one of the night guards. "Didn't expect to see you tonight. You're not on call."

"No." He couldn't very well explain the real reason he was here anyhow. Jim had a wife and two kids at home. He wouldn't understand what was left when a long-term commitment fell apart. He had been with Sarah since college. She had been his anchor during most of his adult life. He had to face facts. Maybe part of the reason he felt adrift was because he was without her.

"I came to check on Whitney Harpswell." That was the truth, too. While she was no longer in his care, he was rooting for her. "I hear she's been more responsive."

"So I hear. It's a hopeful sign," Jim agreed.

The corridors were quieter in the evening. The dinner trays had been served and cleared, and most patients were asleep or nearly so. Visitors were gone.

That is, Mike reminded himself, except for a few. He stopped in the hall outside Harpswell's door. Her husband was still in there, his voice a long rumble. He was talking to her, or reading something. Reading something, he decided by the steady cadence of those mumbling words.

He went to clear his throat, to announce his presence, and he overheard. He didn't mean to. Sounded like Harpswell was reading the Bible.

Best not to focus on that. Relying on anyone, even God, wasn't his thing. What did strike him was the husband's sincerity and tender regard for his wife as he stopped reading to brush a finger against the side of her face and pressed a kiss there.

Commitment and devotion, Mike understood those things. But there was no reserve in the husband's gaze. No embarrassment in showing his affections for his wife. No mistaking the man's emotions as he folded his hands, bowed his head and blinked back tears.

I waited for you. Sarah's words came back to him,

not taunting, not angry, and with all the notes of despair that had been in her voice. *With every deployment, I was right here carrying my cell everywhere in case you had time to call. I loved you enough to wait.*

He had no doubt that if he had been hurt serving his country, Sarah would have been sitting at his bedside, refusing to leave, just the way John Harpswell was with his wife.

Mike cleared his throat and grabbed the chart. "Good evening, Harpswell."

"Major." He straightened, startled.

"Don't bother to salute. This is a social call." A new one for him. He flipped open the chart, studying the chicken scratch. "She opened her eyes twice today. That's good progress."

"She recognized me and talked a little."

"It's not uncommon for a coma patient to move in and out of consciousness." Mike took in the young soldier's stance. There was a man who fought for his woman, whatever it took. Mike felt like a failure in comparison. A big, know-nothing failure. That was a tough thing for a surgeon to admit. He replaced the chart. "I have a good feeling that Whitney is going to pull through this."

Harpswell gave a nod, struggling with emotion. The kid looked tired. He had to be early twenties, and yet the weariness made him look older. His devotion to his wife made him look stronger. He studied his wife and laid his hand on the Bible on his knee. "I'm sure a man like you has seen more than a few miracles. It's awesome, how God can work through us. I'm grateful to you for recognizing her when she was brought in."

"I'm glad to help."

"Probably just another miracle to you, but they are rare for me. Thank you, sir."

Emotion burned like acid reflux, making it hard to answer. "You're welcome. I'll check in again tomorrow."

Since he had two patients in ICU, he made a quick walk through, noticed a young army wife pale with worry fighting tears and he asked one of the nurses about her. Just as he suspected. She belonged with one of his patients. He gave her permission to stay with her young husband as long as his vitals remained stable. He was seeing things differently tonight and he hated to think of the reason.

It was because of Sarah.

You were always promising, and I was always waiting. Her honesty haunted him as he retraced his steps through the quiet corridors. *I was never the woman you were going to open your heart to.*

She was just plain wrong. He should have told her that, he thought as he hiked through the automatic doors and into the crisp December night. The temperature was falling, and his breath rose in clouds as he pulled his keys from his pocket. Not only was Sarah wrong, she was rewriting history. He loved her one hundred percent. He was faithful to her. He was committed to her. He had never let anyone as close to him as he had let Sarah.

He unlocked his doors and climbed behind the

wheel. In the moment between inserting his key and turning the ignition, a seed of doubt took root. Sure, he had let Sarah closer to him than anyone, but what if she was right? What if he hadn't let her close enough?

He thought of John Harpswell and the young army wife in the waiting room. If Sarah had been the one in ICU, would he have sat the whole night through waiting for her?

Sure he would. He backed out of his space and tooled through the lot. He had been devoted to Sarah. A man didn't have to get teary-eyed and emotional to be in love with a woman.

That was someplace he wouldn't go, even for Sarah. He didn't do emotion. Not when he'd lost his brother, killed during Desert Storm. Not when he lost his mom. Even standing by his father's grave as a boy, watching his mother receive the American flag in honor, he hadn't shed a tear. He'd grown up that way. Lots of people had.

Although he supposed his career choice only accentuated his long-standing reserve. Being cold and clinical, it was what made him good at what he did. But he wasn't uncaring.

No, Sarah wasn't right. She couldn't be. He turned the wheel toward the duplex—home now. The trouble was, it didn't feel like home. He thought of the empty rooms with a few pieces of furniture. No, the only place that did these days was a little yellow house across town. Sarah's place.

"She's not right," he told himself, but alone in his car, not even the darkness answered.

Chapter Ten

❧

"Ali, you are supposed to be standing still." Sarah repositioned her camera. She was having a little trouble keeping her subject in focus. "You're hopping up and down again."

"But I wanna see the lights." He twisted around and stared up the length of the newly decorated tree. "They're all flashy."

"Isn't that just special?" She was more of a non-flashing light girl, but she didn't mind the constant on and off of what had to be two thousand lights.

Okay, so she had gone a little overboard in the store with Ali, but his elation and wonder was exactly what Christmas should be. This was, after all, a blessed season and doubly so because of the child in her care.

"I'm still waiting to take this picture," she gently reminded him. She needed him to stand still for two seconds. "Now smile."

Ali posed, eyes wide with wonder on his round,

sweet face. She clicked just in time. Another second and he was struggling not to squirm again, his little-boy excitement getting the best of him.

"Know what, Sarah?"

She laughed. Really, she had heard that phrase how many times today? A dozen? Two dozen? It felt like a hundred. She set her camera down on the mantel, well out of danger of being accidentally knocked to the floor. "What?"

"I sure wish Mike could see this." Ali clasped his hands together, gazing up at the white light of the angel on the tippy top. "I think he would like it lots."

"I think so, too." She thought of what Olga had recommended, to reassure Ali those he loved may be out of sight but not out of reach, and remembered what Mike had said tonight in her kitchen. They were united in this purpose of helping Ali through his grief. "We could send him a picture over the phone."

"Okay!" Ali hopped, all excitement. "Then can I call Mike?"

"After we send him the picture. I can think of a problem, and it's going to be a big one." She winked at him as she went to the sofa table and plucked her cell from the outer pocket. "I'm gonna need your help. You are going to have to stand still for the pictures."

He giggled. "But I got too much happy."

"Me, too." She dropped a kiss on his forehead before kneeling down. She angled her phone to get the best shot. She took four pictures before she was able to get Ali in a still pose. She kept the other pictures to send to

Mike. He might appreciate how cute Ali looked awash with the jeweled glow from the lights and full of awe as he took in all the colors and ornaments.

"Did you send 'em?" Ali popped to her side. He understood the process, since she often sent cute, impromptu pics to her mom.

"I'm all ready." She hit Mike's cell number and sent one picture after another. "There, let's go outside. Don't forget your coat!"

Ali skidded to a stop at the door, his hand on the knob. Clarence lifted his head from the back of the couch cushion, keeping an eye on things.

"Oops." He backtracked and yanked his coat down from the closet. The hanger went flying. "Uh-oh."

She laughed. Someone was doing better. That was what mattered. "Don't worry about it. Zip all the way up, and don't forget your hat."

"My hat!" Ali pulled it out of his coat pocket and yanked it onto his head.

She felt as bright as the lights flashing on the tree and as hopeful as the season as she grabbed her camera and fetched her coat. On her way out the door, she turned the inside lights off and followed her boy out into the yard. The outside strings were flashing cheerfully, so the tree in the window was a fitting addition.

She wanted to capture everything she could of this night and keep it in a scrapbook to treasure forever. The sparkle of glass snowflakes dangling from the tree's branches. The cold, crisp December smell in the air that was a mix of nighttime and hope. The little boy embracing the dance of multicolor lights. She wanted to remember forever the joy in her heart as Ali took her hand.

"It's so pretty," he said, gazing up at the impressive display of lights.

Joy was everywhere. The brush of the crisp breeze against her face. The presence of this little boy in her life. The distant twinkle of stars in the black-velvet sky. God is gracious indeed, she acknowledged, letting the beauty of the season take her over.

This was about love. She had never felt the power of God's presence so clearly. Love, she realized, and knelt down to snuggle the child in her care, for all children were God's children.

There it went again. Mike pulled to a stop, cut the engine and grabbed his phone. He had six messages from Sarah. He hit Read before he could think about it.

Ali's shining face smiled up at him from the screen. Joy filled Ali's big brown eyes and made his grin impossibly wide. The tree they had picked out together was in the background, lit and decorated. The caption read, *There aren't enough lights, Sarah.*

He chuckled. He could picture how that must have gone. He had never seen a tree with so many lights wrapped around one branch. That was Sarah, all charm and twinkle lights. She kept a string above her top kitchen cabinets all year round, the white kind that didn't flash, because they made her think of angel lights, she'd told him. Another set was strung up over her bookshelves in the third bedroom she used as a library, and another set slung over the curtain rods in that same room.

Why he was smiling and remembering, he couldn't rightly say. He grabbed his gym bag, not that he had made it to the gym today, and marched into the duplex. He hit the lights, dropped the bag and hit Next.

Can I call Mike yet? Sarah had captioned the image of Ali, hands clasped together in mid-hop. Classic. Mike had seen that pose before. His chest was expanding, pressing against his ribcage.

He selected the next message and wasn't disappointed. Apparently in his hopping, Ali had knocked an ornament to the floor. Sarah had caught the shot as he knelt down to inspect the fallen wooden soldier, a sheepish grin on his face. *Did I do that?* she'd written.

He missed Sarah's sweet humor.

His phone rang. Was she thinking of him, too? "Hello?"

"Mike!" Ali's voice singsonged through the airwaves. "Did you get 'em?"

"The pictures? Yeah, buddy. They're great." He headed to the fridge. "You and Sarah did a fantastic job with the tree."

"I know! I hanged the soldiers."

"I figured." He grabbed a can of iced tea from the door. "Did you see the outside one?"

"I'm looking at it right now." He scrolled ahead and there it was. Ali standing on the porch, awash in the glow of Christmas, looking more like himself. "All those lights are pretty cool."

"I know! Know what?"

Mike chuckled. "What?"

"I saved some lights for you." The boy sounded so proud of himself.

"Are you telling me that you had lights left over? You and Sarah must have bought out the store."

"Nope, there were boxes left. When can I come?"

"Uh, I'm not sure."

"You got a tree yet?"

Mike popped the top of the tea and took a cooling sip.

"No, buddy. I don't have a tree yet."

"I could help you. I pick good trees."

"I can't argue with you there." He came to a stop outside the second bedroom, vacant and dark.

How did he explain to the kid that Christmas was just another day to him this year.

His pager beeped. Work calling him. Mike knew he had to wrap this up. "How about we talk about this tomorrow, Ali?"

By the time he ended the call, he realized he hadn't talked to Sarah. He called in—there had been a night-training accident and a soldier was on the way—he didn't have time to so much as text her a thanks.

Maybe it was for the best.

He grabbed his keys, killed the lights and locked the door behind him.

Mike. Sarah knew she shouldn't be thinking about him during Pastor Fields's closing prayer, but whenever she opened her heart her affection for him was there, stubbornly unyielding.

Help me, please, Lord. Please take this love from my heart. She felt cold inside, asking for such a thing. She didn't know what else to do. Last night she had lain awake long into the night, going over everything Mike had said.

Is that what I did to you? Did I keep you at arm's length? From the expression on his face, he had looked puzzled, as if he couldn't understand. Mike was a good man; he hadn't intentionally kept her at arm's length. He hadn't made promises to her or Ali that he intended to break. From his view, he had done his best. It was time to forgive him and let go of his failings and her own.

The closing hymn broke into her thoughts. Mom, who had driven down from Austin, was holding the hymnal open for them both. Ali was humming along, and as the sunlight spilled through the magnificent stained-glass windows, she saw a movement in the corner of her eye.

Mike. He stood in the doorway, hands in his jacket pockets, shoulders squared, looking like the outstanding soldier he was. Her soul sighed. The last thing she wanted was to feel any reaction for this man whatsoever.

The length of the sanctuary vanished. The singing silenced. They seemed alone, with no distance between them. She could see beyond the exhaustion on his face to his weary spirit beneath, and deeper, to the grief within. He was troubled. Everything within her longed to go to him and hold him until he no longer felt so alone. Love for this man shone like a beacon in her and it took all her strength of will to remain rooted to the floor and finish the last chorus.

He's here, Lord. He's standing in this church. Isn't

that the first step? She prayed with all her might. *Please help him.*

The hymn ended; the service was over. Conversation broke out, the pleasant din echoing above the rustle of movement and the shuffle as worshippers began making their way to the doors.

"What a nice church this is," Mom commented. "I'm glad you have a family here."

"I truly do. God has been very gracious. While I have you and Dad, I couldn't have a more wonderful family, He has blessed my life to bring even more wonderful people into my family." She stepped into the aisle and realized that Ali was standing still, listening intently. She held out her hand. "Come on, sweetie."

Ali trudged forward. "Sarah? Do you know what?"

Sarah bit her lip, trying not to laugh. "What?" she asked for what felt like the thousandth time.

"You're my family." He placed his hand in hers. "You and Nanny Alice."

"That's right, Ali." She knelt down right in the middle of the crowded main aisle and pulled him to her. She loved that his arms wrapped around her neck so tightly. "Do you know who I saw by the door a moment ago?"

"Who?" Ali let go, eyes bright. "Pastor Fields? Santa Claus?"

"Mike." Sarah bit her lip again. It didn't help that her mom was silently laughing.

"I knew he come." Ali grinned, marching forward. "Are you comin', too, Sarah?"

That wasn't a trick question, was it? She wondered

as she hurried to keep up. "Only as far as the door. You and Mike need your boy time."

"You came ice skating with us." Confused, Ali turned around, walking backward.

Sarah gently steered him by the shoulder so he wouldn't knock into anyone. She watched her mom's surprised reaction. Before her mom could even ask if there was a chance for her and Mike, she shook her head. "No, sorry, Mom. Ali is the reason I see Mike at all."

"You don't like Mike?" That was Ali, smile fading. "How come?"

"I like Mike just fine." This is where it got tricky. Ali was watching, Mom was listening and there was Mike leaning against the wall next to the door, within earshot. "There he is."

"Mike." Ali ran the last few steps toward his hero. "Do you know what we *gotta* do?"

"I have no idea, but I bet you're going to tell me." Mike smiled, and it warmed his eyes. It didn't chase the exhaustion from his face or the shadows lurking there, but it was remarkable.

The tension knotted in every muscle eased a notch. She blushed, realizing that she was smiling right back at him. "Hi, Mike."

"Sarah, you're looking good. Hello, Alice. It's been a long time."

"Yes it has, Mike. You're looking well." Mom went right up to Mike and gave him a brief, motherly hug. "I prayed for you every day you were over there. I'm glad you're home safe."

"Thanks, Alice. It's good to see you again. How's Fred?"

"Probably with his feet up in his lounger watching his favorite sports channel."

"Please tell him howdy from me." Mike ruffled Ali's dark hair. "Are you ready for our big day?"

"Yes! I got it all figured out."

"Do you, now? I'm glad. I was at the hospital until an hour ago." He felt Sarah's concern like a touch to his face. He didn't want to be aware of her, so he turned toward the door. "How about we grab a bite first?"

"Pizza." Ali led the way down the steps.

"You got it, buddy." Mike hated that even walking away from her, his senses were filled with her. Her footsteps padding behind him down the stairs. The whisper of her coat hem snapping in the wintry breeze. The low, beautiful tones of her voice as she spoke with Alice.

When his boots touched grass, he halted and she filled his vision with her sleek red hair and wholesome beauty. She was wearing the green dress he liked so well, that brought out the jewel blue of her eyes. He forced his attention on the boy at his side.

"Sarah, I might not make it through the evening."

"Then just let me know and I'll come get him." She glanced behind him at the church steps. "It's no problem."

"I appreciate that." In full sunlight, he looked ashen. Exhaustion hollowed his eyes and cheekbones. His stance was straight, his shoulders were back, he walked with strength. He was a man who never showed his weaknesses. "C'mon, kid, let's head for my truck."

"I sure wish Sarah and Nanny Alice could come." Ali's sweet voice carried as he trailed alongside Mike. Man and boy trudged off together, and anyone watching would think they belonged together. There was just something about the two of them that matched.

"Mike could have fought you for him," Mom pointed out with that know-all tone of hers.

She meant well. Sarah had to remember that. She watched the man and boy against the green grass and blue sky and told herself she wasn't pining after Mike. She was not that kind of girl. She wouldn't allow it. She was free of him now and of the past. She was moving on.

Then why did her spirit follow him like the moon and the earth?

You have to stop loving him, she told herself firmly. "Mike is too busy. He would never give up his commitment to his work and to the army. That's probably why he didn't fight for Ali."

Even as she said the words they didn't ring true. Down deep, she couldn't believe it. Mike wasn't that cold. It would be easier for her to move on with her life if he was. If only life and love were simpler. "C'mon, Mom. I want to introduce you to Olga Terenkov and her daughter, Anna. Anna runs Children of the Day, you know, the place where I volunteer?"

"Oh, yes, they were the agency that brought little Ali over from the Middle East." Mom looked pleased. "Yes, I want to thank them for all they have done for my grandson."

"The adoption hasn't gone through."

"It will. Think positively, sweetheart." Mom drew her close. "God has a way of making life come out right. Now come and introduce me."

"Sure." She stopped to watch Mike's pickup rolling down the street.

You don't love him, she told herself, but it was a lie.

Chapter Eleven

Mike was dragging, glad the kid needed a nap. He shook the light blanket over the couch, covering up Ali completely. He waited for the boy to start giggling.

"Mike! Mike! I'm under here."

He lifted back one edge of the blanket to reveal Ali's round face. "Oh, there you are. I thought I had lost you for a minute there."

"Nope. I got all covered up." He gave a wide yawn. "I'm not sleepy."

"Too bad, because I am." He tucked the blanket well, cocooning the little guy. He looked snug and warm. "Just close your eyes for fifteen minutes, and then you can get up."

"Why?"

"Because I need fifteen minutes of shut-eye."

"I need fifteen minutes of shut-eye, too." Ali closed his eyes.

Mike wasn't fooled. The kid was paying attention to

his every movement. He kicked off his boots and set his watch to go off in fifteen. The recliner sure felt good. He eased back and put his feet up. Fifteen minutes would be long enough to get him through the rest of the afternoon and short enough that he probably wouldn't slip into a nightmare. With any luck.

He closed his eyes, and what did he see? Sarah. Standing there with the sun bronzing her hair and surrounded by life, by the people she loved. She looked different somehow, more at peace. She was a dream that was no longer his. Why was his chest aching like this? Why was it hard to breathe? He no longer loved her. He had not been at fault.

I loved you enough to wait. He could still hear her broken heart in those words. No, he argued. She hadn't waited. She had been the problem. Not him.

Because if it had been him, he couldn't deal with that. He could handle a lot of things. He could handle war, and shot-up soldiers and patching up one trauma wound after another all the night long. What he couldn't take was being the reason he had lost Sarah. She was the best thing that had ever happened to him.

You've got to slow down, Mike. Breathe deep. He drew a chest full of air before he realized the shallow, panicked breathing he heard wasn't his.

Ali. Mike's eyes snapped open and he sat up in the chair. The little boy's brow was damp and he was thrashing beneath the blanket. He shot out of the chair.

"Sarah! Sarah, no. Sar-ah." Ali's cry came tortured.

Mike was on his knees, wrapping the little boy in his

arms, gently rocking him awake. "Hey, it's okay, Ali. You're safe now."

"M-Mike." Arms wrapped around his neck and held on. "I had a bad dream."

"I see that." He felt hot tears against his neck. The boy in his arms was trembling. "You're all right, little buddy. Just take a deep breath."

"I l-lost Sa-rah." Ali gulped in a mouthful of air. "We was at the store and I couldn't f-find her. I looked and looked."

He didn't have to be a psychologist to know what that meant. Mike sat down on the couch and drew the blanket around Ali, to keep him warm and comforted. "You're afraid that you might lose Sarah the way you lost your mom?"

"She said she isn't going to leave me."

"If Sarah said it, she means it. I would believe her." But they both knew Ali's mother hadn't wanted to leave him, either. Mike was at a loss. He didn't know what to say. He wasn't prepared for this and he was too tired to think straight. "You listen to me, ya hear?"

Ali nodded, growing solemn, tears still spilling from his eyes.

He hoped to high Heaven he was going to say this right. "Things are different this time. Do you know why?"

Ali shook his head.

"Because you've got family all around you." Mike grabbed his shirtsleeve to wipe the kid's face. It was all he had available. "You've got Sarah, and you've got Alice."

"Nanny Alice and Papa Fred." Ali gave a little sigh.

"Papa Fred likes sports, too, and he barbecues hot dogs. And Aunt Claire and Uncle Tim."

"See?" Mike imagined Sarah's family, who were kind and decent people, would have taken time to get to know Ali. "That's five people in your family right there. And you have all the folks who helped you at Children of the Day."

"And Olga." The tension began to ease out of him. "She helps me."

"And what about the church you go to?" He might not need religion, but he respected the work Franklin Fields did at his church. Their paths had crossed many times at the hospital. "You have friends and people who are like family there, right?"

"Yep." Ali clapped his hands together.

"Right."

"And I've got you, Mike."

"You've got me." Mike brushed a kiss on the crown of Ali's head. He and the kid weren't going to be family, but then family was more than legal papers and blood ties. "I'm not going to let anything happen to you."

"Or Sarah."

"Or Sarah." It wasn't a lie. It was the truth. Maybe the only truth he had ever known.

Come for Ali at six. That was all Mike's text message had said. She hesitated on the walkway outside his duplex, not knowing what to expect. His message had been to the point, but she remembered how he had looked in the churchyard. She had never seen him so wrung out. He was so committed to the army he never stopped giving.

The trick was to keep control of her feelings. She ambled up the concrete steps onto the dark porch. She had to act as if she had moved on. Maybe the act of doing so would make it true eventually. It was worth a try.

There were no lights up. No Christmas decorations. No personal effects of any kind. Sarah knocked, smiling when she heard the muffled tap of Ali's shoes. The door swung open and Ali flew into her arms.

"Sarah!"

"I'm glad to see you, too!" She felt Mike's gaze on her. He stood behind the door, holding it open. "Hi, Mike. If you'll hand over his coat, I'll get out of your way—"

"Actually, I hoped you had a minute." His baritone rang unsure. There was a plea in his eyes. "I need to talk to you."

About Ali. She could tell that's what he meant. "All right—"

"Come in, Sarah!" Ali tugged her over the threshold, dangerously close to Mike.

Don't remember what it was like to be in his arms, she ordered herself. *Don't remember how safe it felt to be held against his chest.* She moved beyond him into the living room, where it felt safer.

Whatever happened, she could not let him think she was pining after him. She had had enough of Mike Montgomery's rejection. She crossed her arms over her chest like a barrier. "What can I do for you, Mike?"

"Come into the kitchen." He closed the door, all stone. It was impossible to read him. "Ali, I would appreciate it if you could finish your picture for my refrigerator."

"I'm gonna make two pictures." Ali rushed to the side table Mike had set up like a desk in front of the couch. His sneakers pounded on the brown carpeting.

Sarah took in the new furniture, brown and beige to match the duplex's interior. There were no mementos. None of the old family pictures he usually hung up. Not a book. Not a CD player. Nothing but the dark television on the floor in the corner. Had he left most things in storage? She shivered. This wasn't the Mike she knew at all.

"I've got tea steeping." He used his doctor tone, impersonal and dispassionate.

She couldn't answer him. It was as if every word she knew evaporated. She could only follow the stranger into the kitchen. The overhead fluorescent lighting was harsh. It unforgivably showed every line carved into his handsome face, every hollow and shadow.

Poor Mike. He might have every shield up, but she could see the nicks in them, the dings and the dents. Something had hurt him very much. She wanted to go to him and rub the tension from his shoulder blades. She wanted to comfort him with kindness and caring until he felt he could confide in her. Longing filled her soul. Love flooded her spirit. Every fiber of her being ached for him.

Remember, you're not supposed to love him, Sarah. She took a step into the kitchen toward a plain white mug on the counter. Mike had set out honey for her and a spoon.

He remembered how she liked her tea. She steadied her hands and squeezed a dollop of honey into her mug.

She could see Ali busy at work on his drawings. His head was bent over his paper, his dark brown hair falling forward and he swiped a blue crayon back and forth, as if making a sky.

Mike picked up the TV remote from the counter and aimed it at the screen. The news blared to life, reporting the weather. A cold front was sweeping in from the north. Mike looked colder, speaking in a quiet tone so Ali wouldn't hear. "Why didn't you tell me he was having nightmares?"

She blinked; she hadn't been expecting that. "Did he have one when he was here?"

A terse nod. That was all. The intimidating soldier stared at her, expectant.

She was at a loss. "It's not that uncommon for children who have gone through the trauma he has."

"He didn't have them when he was with me." His flat tone gave nothing away, except anger. He definitely sounded angry. But standing military straight without moving a single muscle, he was more like anger coiled and waiting.

Was he accusing her? She kept her voice low, so her words wouldn't carry. "That's the way post traumatic stress works. You know that, Mike. It often manifests after the event when the person feels safe again. Believe it or not, it's a good sign, at least in a way. He's feeling safe. Now he can work through his grief issues and his fears. He's healing."

"You should have told me." A tendon beat in his neck.

"Told you?" She was at a complete and utter loss. The man towering over her as cold as ice was not the Mike she had known for so long. "What happened to you over there?"

A muscle tensed along his jaw line. "I don't want to talk about it."

"Maybe you need to." Against every instinct and every warning, she laid her hand on his forearm. The instant her fingers met his arm, the old connection zinged to life between them.

Maybe he felt that, too. "I lost a lot of good soldiers."

That was all. Nothing. No elaboration.

Mike wasn't used to losing. She wished she could comfort him. Her hand remained on his arm, and the tension in his muscles increased. That was Dr. Montgomery, cool and calm in the face of any tragedy. He was still in that mode, she realized. He had lost patients before, any trauma surgeon had to face that from time to time. "Mike, if you couldn't save them, then no one could."

He blinked, his only reaction. "You weren't there."

His flat, harsh tone was like a slap. She took a sip of tea, breathing in the steam and the sweet goodness, wondering if it was *her* sympathy he didn't want, or any sympathy at all.

"No, I wasn't there," she conceded. "But you give everything you have to the soldiers who come to your MASH unit. You don't hold back."

"Don't patronize me. You don't understand."

"I see." Her hand shook. She put the cup down on

the counter. Tea sloshed over the side. Mike had never spoken to her that way before. Rattled, she searched for a dishcloth or a paper towel, but there was nothing but the bare length of counters.

"Leave it," he clipped out. "Is there anything else you want to tell me about Ali? Anything I should know about?"

She willed her eyes to his. Grief shadowed his face. Grief for the men and women he hadn't been able to save? She feared she would never know. She wanted to help him, but there were so many reasons why it wasn't a good idea. And only one why it was.

"Only that he needs you. I know you want to move on with your life, and that you are spending time with him for his sake." Again, no reaction. She swallowed, weighing her words. "But he needs more than that from you. Maybe you do, too. There's no reason why you can't pick him up after school or after his day care. That way you never have to see me."

"You're ad-dopting him." His hard tone broke on the word, the only betrayal of his stoic front.

"Ali needs all the family he can get. You brought hope into his life. I think it is only right that he brings the same to yours."

"I'm not—" His jaw tightened with defensiveness.

Footsteps pounded in their direction, and Mike fell silent. He visibly melted at the sight of the little boy tripping into the room, waving a paper for them to see.

"Look what I did!" Ali skidded to a stop, his work of art twisting in his wake. "You gotta see, Mike."

"What do you have there?" He leaned forward to take a peek.

Ali's artwork was five-year-old skill, but Mike could make out two people, a tall one dribbling what had to be a basketball while the smaller one defended the hoop. Pressure built in his throat.

"It's you and me." Ali leaned close. "That was when I winned."

"I see that." Mike fought emotion, remembering. "That was when I taught you to shoot hoops."

"Yep." Ali sighed contentedly. "You gonna put it on your fridgerator?"

"You know it. I've got tape right here." He whipped open the junk drawer and pulled the dispenser from its place in the drawer organizer. With every passing second he could feel Sarah watching him. He could feel her curiosity and probably her censure. He moved by rote, fighting to hold the threatening emotions at bay. "Where should I put this masterpiece?"

"Right here." Ali patted the flat of his hand in the center of the door.

"Excellent spot." He tore off four strips of tape and stuck them to the corners of Ali's drawing. He let the little guy stick it up, after all, he was the artist. But the truth was, it hurt too much to look at that rendering.

He hadn't realized it until now. Sarah was right.

"We gonna have dinner yet?" Ali broke into his thoughts, staring up at him with endless trust in his dark eyes.

I don't need anyone, Mike told himself. Looking at the boy standing in front of the picture he'd drawn of them, it wasn't need beating at the armor guarding his heart. No, never that. He was too strong to need anyone. But it didn't hurt to have a little company now and then. And it wasn't as if he had to figure out the future right this minute.

"If it's all right with Sarah, I can whip up something." He tried to sound casual, but it was difficult. "How about spaghetti?"

"I only like it with short noodles." Ali grinned.

Short noodles? He arched his brow, looking over the top of the boy's head to where Sarah stood, quiet and serene with more emotion than he wanted to analyze as soft as light on her lovely face.

"I break up the noodles before I cook them," she explained in her gentle way.

She ought to be angry with him, the way he had ambushed her. He hadn't meant to, but he could see that now, too. He didn't know what was wrong with him. This wasn't like him. He swiped a hand over his face, trying to pull it together.

"You two take it easy in the living room. I'll get cooking. How's that?" The least he could do was fix her a meal.

"Sorry, that's unacceptable." She waltzed toward him, impossibly kind, and his world brightened. It was as if she brought the light with her. "You look exhausted, Mike, but I can tell you aren't going to let me do the cooking."

"You got that right." The corner of his mouth

twitched. He wasn't trying to smile. Really. "But if you accept my apology, I'll let you help."

"You've got yourself a deal, Dr. Montgomery." When Sarah smiled, the world seemed a little more beautiful.

Chapter Twelve

So much had changed, Sarah reflected, as she found a deep-sided pan in a lower cabinet. She and Mike used to cook together all the time, but it had never been as quiet between them as this. Mike had changed. She wanted to talk to him about that more, but he looked closed off and remote again. Unreachable as he peeled an onion and began slicing with accurate, swift strokes of the blade.

She measured out olive oil, grappling with what to say. He had his back solidly to her. Did she ask him about his work? How he was adjusting to being back on U.S. soil? Or was it better to leave the uncomfortable silence between them?

"Did Alice head home?"

"Yes." She capped the bottle and set it in the top cabinet. "We went Christmas shopping for a certain little boy, and she left around four. She wanted to be home in time to fix supper for Dad."

"She looks happy to finally have a grandchild."

"She and Dad adore Ali." She pulled measuring spoons from the nearby drawer. It was better to concentrate on measuring the fresh herbs Mike had just chopped than to let herself think about the man. "Oh, I have more family news. You know my little sister was married last year."

"Yes." The one word was cold and clipped.

She knew very well that he knew. It had been during the reception at Claire's wedding that Mike had decided to tell her he was thinking about staying in the army. That discussion had led to their breakup. "She's expecting in June."

"Well, give her my congratulations."

"I will."

It felt wrong, this small talk when there was so much between them. She couldn't pretend they were strangers. She couldn't pretend not to care. Did he feel that way, too? She measured the sweet smelling basil and oregano into a small bowl.

"I didn't ask about the charity fund-raiser. I suppose it will be the same time same place as always?"

"Yes, on New Year's Eve at the skating rink. It's the perfect family event." She was a cochair on the fund-raising committee. "I'm in charge of the invitations and press announcements."

"Good. It's a good cause."

"It is." She thought of children all over the world the charity had helped, just like Ali. "Mike, it's none of my business, but I have to ask. Are you all right?"

"Sure, why?" He carried the loaded cutting board to the stove and swept the minced onion into the pan. "I'm a little tired, but I worked all night."

"I know you did." She measured parsley, watching as Mike retreated to the counter where he attacked a few cloves of garlic. His shoulders were tensed again and seemed as wide as the Texas sky. He was such a good man, noble of heart and dedicated in all the ways that counted. She could see that more than ever. "I'm sure the soldier's family is grateful to you, Mike."

"You don't know the particulars of the case." He sounded defensive.

She hadn't meant to put him there. "I know that he was fortunate to have a gifted surgeon like you."

"I'm a doctor, Sarah. Helping people is what I do." His knife worked with fast, short strokes.

"Yes it is, and I admire that about you." Her voice was quiet, but the meaning behind them was not. "It matters what you do. You make a difference in this world, Mike. That's why I decided to be a foster parent. I wanted to make a difference. I believe that's one reason why God put us on this earth."

"So, you've turned real religious, huh?" He carried the cutting board with him and emptied it into the pan.

"Yes. I'm a believer now. I was tiptoeing around for a while, you remember."

He didn't answer. He put the board in the sink, trying to figure her out. So much had changed about her, and yet, from what he could tell those changes had only made her more *Sarah* than ever. More sweetness and goodness and caring. She was everything good in the world—and, once, in his world.

Part of him wished she could be again.

"After I saw you board that plane, I had never felt so alone." She had turned the stove on and was digging a wooden spoon out of the drawer.

He hated to think of her alone. He knew just what she meant. She had been his center. His life. She had accused him of being more committed to the army, but she was his anchor. She was his shoulder to lean on and his soft place to fall. Without her to reach out to, the first month away had been hard to weather.

"I was alone, too," he admitted. "I hadn't been there a full day when we were hammered. The roadside bombings, convoy attacks and an offensive surge brought in more casualties. I don't think I slept through a single night for a month."

The pan was sizzling and Sarah turned her attention to stirring the onion and garlic, but he could feel her listening. He just needed to talk about it; maybe that was why he kept going. "There were so many civilians this time. Old and young. Women and babies. And the soldiers, they keep getting younger every year. It took a toll."

"I can see that, Mike."

He figured everyone could. He sure could every time he looked in the mirror. He rinsed the cutting board and knife and stuck them in the dishwasher. It gave him enough time to gather up his words and debate if he wanted to say more or not.

Sarah kept stirring, her back to him, but it was as if her spirit was leaning toward him, listening in her compassionate way. He knew for a fact there were places on this earth and people in it who did not care who they hurt or how. He felt damaged by being exposed to so much of that world. He wanted to put his arms around Sarah and draw her close and breathe in her goodness and her innocence. To once again dwell in her life of sunshine and children's picture books and kindness.

"A month after Ali left we found ourselves under attack."

"I hadn't heard." Sarah dropped the spoon. It clattered to a rest against the steel side of the pan. When she covered her face, her hands were shaking. "You never said anything?"

"No. It was a small skirmish. We had some Rangers staying with us, good protection and within minutes air support. It happens."

She looked so upset. Her hands dropped away to reveal tears in her eyes. "You weren't hurt?"

"No." He blotted out the images of the mortar hitting the edge of the camp. He fought down the sound of the explosion and the strike of flying shrapnel and debris. A nurse's scream of terror. The shouts of agony. How he had jumped off his cot and headed into the action with his rifle and his medical kit.

"Mike?" Her hand was on his chest. He didn't know how it had gotten there or when she had crossed over to him. He could still hear the rat-tat-tat of machine gun fire and see the blood all around him.

"Mike? Have you talked to someone about this?"

"No." How did he tell her that it had always only been her. Just her. He had no one else. Embarrassed, hating the weakness that was taking him over, he tried to step away.

He wasn't strong enough. He needed her sympathy and her comfort just for a few moments. Just long enough to get past this. Maybe then he could stand on his own two feet. Maybe then he could go back to not needing anyone.

"Ben, one of the Rangers who protected us, was hit and hit bad. I did everything I could for him. Everything—" He stopped short, knowing she couldn't understand. Sometimes his best was enough. Sometimes it wasn't. "Ben had a wife and two small boys. I failed him—"

"You don't control life and death, Mike." Her hand on his chest felt like comfort. Her words tempted him with peace.

That was the easy way out. He stepped back, gathering up the pieces of himself. He glanced over the counter to see Ali busily coloring, blissfully unaware of the serious discussion.

"You had better get that pan back on the heat," he said, trying not to be terse, trying not to be cold and distant. "I'll get the diced tomatoes from the pantry."

"Okay."

Sarah's sympathy was a temptation he had to turn away from. It wasn't until he had the pantry open and was sorting through the few cans on the shelves that it hit him. "You saw my transport plane take off?"

"I was there, Mike." She didn't look up from her stirring, her turn to be distant. "I came to say goodbye."

"I never saw you. I thought you didn't care."

"I couldn't face you. I couldn't let you know how much I still loved you." She said nothing more, stirring away.

He knew her well enough to recognize the tense line of her jaw and the way her soft lips had clamped together. There were things she didn't want him to know, emotions she didn't want to show him.

He put the cans on the counter, moving slow, feeling the cracks in his armor. He thought she hadn't cared at all. It mattered that she did. Sure, it was too late for them, but it helped to know that he wasn't wrong in how deeply he had once loved her.

Mike's story stuck with her as she set the table. She watched him out of the corner of her eye. He stood peeling carrots at the counter next to the bowl of mixed greens. Her soul brightened with a quiet, impossible hope. It was like old times between them, working together to get the meal on the table.

"That's my pager." He pulled it out of his pocket and studied the screen. "It's work. Would you mind finishing up?"

"Sure." She put the final knife and fork in place, straightened the napkins and wove around him to the salad bowl. She took up the peeler, aware of every step he took to the living room, the way he stopped to comment on the finishing touches of Ali's second masterpiece.

Mike would make a great dad one day. He and Ali shared grins as he picked up the cordless extension and hit speed dial.

"Sarah!" Ali dashed around the edge of the counters. "This one's all for you."

"For me? Should it go on our refrigerator, too?"

"Yep." He held up the paper proudly. "It's when we was skatin'. That's you. That's Mike. That's me in the middle."

The block figures with legs and arms and heads were side-by-side, a family. Wishes lost rose from the bottom of her soul. Those dreams moved through her heart sweetly and painfully, like melody and harmony, like dawn when there was both darkness and light, shadow and color.

If she had one Christmas wish, it would be this. That she and Mike could forgive each other for their mistakes and find their way back to one another. That love would save them.

"It's Whitney." Mike was at the counter, striding purposefully, as if he were holding himself up by sheer will. "She's out of her coma. Not just responsive, but sitting up and talking."

"That's wonderful news. An answered prayer." Sarah thought of the young couple and their kind letters to her morning kindergarten class months ago, before they had gone missing during their deployment. "Will she be able to go home in time for Christmas?"

"The chances sound pretty good." Mike looked lighter, as if some of the shadows had abated. "I'm glad when things work out right."

"You had a hand in that." She went to him and laid her hand against his jawline, strong with a firm line of bone and rough with a day's stubble. "You have made a lot of happy endings, Mike. I know the sad ones weigh on you, but look at all the good you have done. All the lives you have helped to save. The families who are whole again because of you."

"That's what I fight so hard for."

She knew. She had always known. It had taken losing him to realize the depth of the goodness he gave to the world. She admired him. She respected him. She loved the man, heart and soul. "It's a battle worth fighting for."

His throat worked and it looked like he wanted to say something. Emotion clouded his eyes, and he looked vulnerable, as if her words had taken down his last defense. He no longer looked remote. "Anyway, you got another picture there, buddy?"

That was Mike, even when he wasn't as closed off, that didn't mean he wanted to talk feelings. But it had been enough, she realized. He had heard what she wanted to say to him. She had learned some hard lessons this past year and some good ones, too. The oven timer beeped.

"I'll get that." It would give Mike time to put his defenses back up—she knew how he was—and he and Ali could admire his drawing. She looked in the stack of drawers for a trivet—typical Mike. Everything was always organized and handy. And popped the pan of crisp, buttery garlic bread onto the stovetop to cool.

The rumble of Mike's deep, kind baritone wrapped around her like a comfy blanket. He was complimenting Ali on his picture, then fell quiet, listening to Ali proudly explaining the details. The occasional "yep," and "uh-huh" was a cozy sound. The dream of him lifted through her like a Christmas carol, gentle and timeless. It had always been this she had dreamed of: The two of them in the kitchen with dinner ready to go on the table. A child or two between them. Happiness in the air.

Like a sign from above, Mike reached into a cabinet and brought down a platter for her. "I'll get the salad," he said.

Did he know how he made her ache with dreams newly remembered? She set the plate of bread on the table, watching as he carried the bowl of salad to the table with Ali at his heels, listening intently to the little boy. He looked all the stronger for his gentleness, a greater man for his unyielding kindness.

Did he know his love was all she had ever wanted? And now, more than that, loving him was beyond all that she wanted for herself. She loved him selflessly, beyond her dreams and all the way to his.

"Mike? When are you gonna get a tree?" Ali put his picture on the edge of the counter. "Are you gonna get a real big one? With lots and lots of lights? Do I getta help? I'm real good at helpin'."

"Hold on there, buddy." Mike's gentle chuckle sounded relaxed and whole, the way it used to. "One question at a time."

"What about the tree? Did you get one yet?" Ali pulled out his chair at the table and climbed up.

"I'm not going to get a tree this year."

Ali's jaw dropped.

Mike headed toward the stove where the pot of spaghetti, sauce and all, was keeping warm on a back burner.

"But Mike, you gotta have a tree. It's *Christmas*."

"I know it's Christmas." Mike took the lid off the spaghetti pot and put it in the sink. He shook his head at Sarah, amused. He had a look on his handsome face that said, I'm having trouble here.

She shrugged. How fun was this? She didn't have any helpful advice for him. She took her chair and waited to see how this would turn out.

"You don't got outside lights."

"I figure I can just look at everyone else's lights." Mike hefted the pot and brought it to the table, where a trivet was waiting in the center of the little square table.

"Oh." Ali didn't look as if he were satisfied with that explanation. "We could get a tree and put it up right there." He pointed at one of the many bare spots in the living room. "So you can see it real good."

"You're real persistent about this tree thing." Mike took his chair.

Biting her bottom lip to keep from laughing, she spread her paper napkin on her lap. No way was he getting out of this.

"We got lights," Ali volunteered. "But I used up all the soldiers."

Including the nutcracker ornaments.

Mike reached for the spaghetti serving spoon.

"Mike, you forgot again." Ali shook his head slowly from side to side, and he couldn't be cuter. "You're supposed to say grace first."

"This is your doing, I'll have you know." Humor sparkled in Mike's hazel eyes as he focused on her—and something else.

Surely that couldn't be approval. Mike wasn't against Christianity, but he didn't embrace it, either. Maybe it was best to keep her tone light. "Should we let Ali say the blessing?"

"I do it real good." Ali bowed his head, already starting. "Dear Father, thank you for the spaghetti and the garlicky bread. Please send a tree with lots of lights for Mike. Amen."

"That's a real good blessing, buddy." He dished up Ali's plate first.

"I know. I want lots."

"No kidding." Mike added another spoonful. "That enough?"

"Nope." Ali shook his head.

Mike added another spoonful. "How about that? Now you've got a spaghetti mountain. I couldn't eat all of that."

There was the Mike she knew. Endless love was like a light in her soul, guiding her and making her see. She knew what he needed. She knew what path God had been leading her on. That path always had been leading her to Mike, and it would always be bringing her back to him.

Ali was giggling, taking up his spoon and waving it in the air as he spoke. "I can eat all of it. And two pieces of bread, too! No, three!"

"Three!" Sarah laughed as she dropped a piece of bread on the side of his plate. "Why don't you start with one first? And don't forget to eat your greens."

"I know. 'Cuz they're healthy." Ali dug in with his spoon, bright with happiness. It was as if he had forgotten about his grief, as if it had sloughed off him like a coat. That was a change, too. A big step on the road to what could be.

"Here, Sarah." Mike was watching her from the other side of the spaghetti pot, holding the loaded serving spoon. "I suppose you want a spaghetti mountain, too?"

"How about a spaghetti foothill. I'm watching my carbs." She debated and took one piece of bread. This meal wasn't helping. She would have an extra-large salad—not that it would help, but she would feel better.

"You look fine, Sarah. Just like always." His voice dipped, rumbling low just as it always did when he was tender with her.

Surely she was reading too much into this? She blushed, afraid to hope. But when she met his eyes, there it was, his steady unblinking scrutiny. He did not look away. Her heart skipped a beat. Every dream she ever had felt on the verge of coming true.

"We have a lot of Christmas parties coming up this week," she explained. "I want to be able to enjoy the goodies and still fit into my jeans."

"We're having a school party!" Ali burst out in mid-bite. "Sarah and me are makin' cupcakes. And we're singing songs. You gonna come, Mike?"

He didn't blink. What was he thinking? Did he feel this, too? Was that tenderness in his gaze? Hope in his heart?

"The school holiday concert," she explained. "You are welcome to come."

"I'll think about it." Mike's smile said he would do more than think about it. "If I'm not working that night."

"Good." Great, she wanted to shout. She wanted to leap up from her chair, skip around the table and wrap her arms around his neck. She wanted to tell him how much she loved him. She wanted to hear that he loved her, too. But she waited, and smiled quietly. This, sharing a cozy evening with conversation and happiness between them, it was more than enough.

It was like Christmas coming early wrapped up in a bright red bow.

Chapter Thirteen

Was the hour up yet? Sarah checked her watch. It wasn't five o'clock yet. She had twelve minutes to go before Ali's counseling session was finished. It had felt like an eternity. She worried about her little boy, of course, but she had someone else on her mind, too. That someone was meeting them here and the three of them were going to walk over to get a bite of supper before the school concert.

"Sarah?" Pastor Franklin Fields broke into her thoughts. "It's good to see you again. Waiting for Ali?"

"Yes. He's in with Olga." Sarah set down her stack of papers—the last ones she would have to grade until school started back in January. Tomorrow was the last day of class. "Are you ready for Christmas?"

"Barely. I'm still working on my Christmas Eve sermon. I trust you and Ali will be there?"

"We wouldn't miss it for the world." Sarah liked the tall, ruggedly handsome pastor. He reminded her a lot of her dad—good heart and truly kind, someone who always did what was right. No wonder Olga was in love with him. "Olga does such fine work here. I hope you appreciate all her wonderful qualities."

"I am well aware of her qualities, yes." There was a little smile in the corners of his mouth. Could it be that the minister was coming around? The two had danced around the issue of love for the last few months. "I noticed Dr. Montgomery came to the last few minutes of Sunday service. I suppose you had something to do with that?"

"No. We were supposed to meet in the parking lot."

"Like I said, I think you had something to do with that." There was that smile again, enigmatic and kind. He opened the door and stepped into the grief center. Sarah caught a glimpse of the brightly painted walls and the room full of toys before the door closed again.

Usually she was comfortable in the hallway, but today she was antsy. No, she was anxious to see Mike again. Things were starting to go very well. Her hopes kept rising. How could they not? They had spoken on the phone twice already this week. The conversations had been pleasant and nothing momentous, but her love for him deepened with each passing day.

She picked up her stack of work and her sheet of gold stars. If only she could stop thinking about Mike. Her thoughts naturally went to him.

She knew the moment when he entered the hallway. Her heart brimmed with feelings too tender and devoted to voice. He ambled down the hall, looking handsome in black jeans, boots and a black sweater underneath his leather jacket.

Be still my heart, she ordered, but it was impossible. This man was her dream come true.

"I'm a few minutes early," he said as he took the empty span of the bench beside her. "There was a lull, and I got out while the gettin' was good. I still have that soldier in I.C.U. I'm keeping an eye on. He's touch and go. He's stable right now, but if that changes again, I'll have to go."

"Absolutely. I've been praying for him. If duty calls you away, I'll let you watch the video of the concert afterward." She gestured to her bag, where her digital recorder was tucked away.

"I've got to say, this is a new attitude for you." He watched her intensely, although he appeared casual and relaxed, as if his words weren't important.

She knew they were. She knew what he meant. "I've done some changing. For the better, I hope."

"If you had it to do over—" He stopped in mid-sentence.

"I would have waited for you." The love in her heart had.

He nodded and said nothing more, but he didn't move away and he didn't draw back. His eyes searched hers, letting her wish, letting her hope.

The grief center door opened and there was Ali. He looked somber as he tumbled into the hallway. "Mike! You're here. I told Olga all about you."

"You did?" Judging by the concerned look on his face,

Mike had noticed Ali's red eyes and tear tracks. "I hope you said only good things. I don't want to get into trouble."

"I said bad stuff." Ali teased, managing a big grin. "How you ate four pieces of garlicky bread. You made a mountain of spaghetti."

"You're right. That is pretty awful. I'll try to behave myself at dinner tonight." Mike ruffled the boy's hair.

"Me, too."

There was no way to mistake the bond between them. Sarah couldn't help adoring both of them. She blinked, realizing she was gawking at both of them. With any luck, Mike hadn't noticed she was staring a little too adoringly. She slid her papers into her bag and stood. "Are you two ready? I'm starving, and Ali, you are going to need some fuel if you are going to sing well tonight."

"I know all the words." Ali took her hand and caught Mike's in his other. He opened his mouth to start singing and stopped. "So, Sarah. What's the first words?"

Yeah, tonight was going to be fun, she thought, and saw the same thought on Mike's face. She helped him out, and he started singing off-key adding a few dance steps. By the time they reached the end of the hall, she and Mike were fighting not to laugh.

"After you, pretty lady." Mike held the door for her, gentlemanly as always.

She brushed past him, unable to look away from him. He was like gravity, holding her in his magnetic pull. She stumbled onto the top step, and that's when she saw the grief center's door swing open and Olga and Franklin Fields walk out together, hand in hand.

One tall, strong silent type down, one to go, Sarah thought as she followed Ali down the steps. She was glad for Pastor Fields. He had taken down his walls of defense and opened up his heart to love. Maybe this time Mike could do the same—truly, without holding back.

They reached the sidewalk and walked along the town green, hand in hand together. Her shoes seemed to be barely touching the ground. She was buoyant with happiness. The bright lights of the shops and the Christmas cheer were decorations on this lovely evening together. The welcoming windows of the Prairie Spring Café drew them from the sidewalk.

"Look up, you two," Max O'Neal called out from behind the counter. "Mistletoe."

"Mistletoe?" Sure enough there was a plastic sprig of it dangling from the light fixture overhead. She blushed and avoided Mike, but she could feel his gaze on her lips, him drawing nearer. His strong, capable hand cupped her jaw tenderly.

"Kiss her!" Max called out. "C'mon."

"Yeah!" One of the diners shouted. "It's tradition."

"Well, if it's tradition," Mike said in his dusty, gentle baritone. "I'm not one to buck doing things the right way."

Her heart dropped two feet. Trembling, she watched Mike lean closer. Warmth softened the hard contours of his face, the way it had when he had once loved her. Had he fallen in love with her again? Her soul ached with the prayer. *Lord, let him love me. Please.*

Mike's lips brushed hers with unmistakable tenderness. He lingered, drawing out the kiss with unfailing reverence. When he pulled away, there was a moment when she could see all the way to his heart.

"I guess we had better get to our table." Mike smiled, genuinely, the shadows vanished.

Only then did she realize that Ali was following Max down the aisle toward a booth and she was standing transfixed, her heart whole once more.

Kissing Sarah. It was all he could think about. Throughout dinner when the three of them were talking and laughing over burgers. Through the walk back to school where he parked next to her vehicle. The three of them. As if they belonged together, just like all the other families streaming into the school's multipurpose room.

When he had dropped Sarah and Ali off in the wings with the music teacher and the other children, he had caught the way Ali was sizing him up. It didn't take a genius to see the wheels turning. The boy had been watching the families, especially the ones with dads. As Ali had waved to him, there had been not just hope in his eyes. There had been certainty. Now, as the kids tromped across the stage and onto the bleachers, Ali was gazing out into the audience, searching.

Mike felt anonymous in the shadowed seats. Safer. He could feel things tugging at him, pulling at the battered walls of his soul. It was because of her kiss. Because he had reached out to her with tenderness. He had been carried away, that's what emotion did to a man, making him feel as if it was okay to open up. That it was okay not to be alone for a while.

And Sarah. She was moving through the semi-dark aisle with her video recorder in hand, searching the rows and rows of folding chairs for him. Oh, she was beauty. She was everything he needed. She always had been. She always would be.

The moment she spotted him, she brightened like the sun. She hurried toward him purposefully, as if he were the only one in the room. When she slipped into the chair beside him, he felt the walls of his defenses crack.

"Look at Ali," she whispered, leaning close, the silk of her hair tickling his jaw.

Sweet, she was so sweet. He needed to lean on her. To put his arm across the back of her chair and tilt just enough in his chair to lay his cheek against her hair, to kiss her forehead and escape from the loneliness and pain that was burdening him.

What he had to be was strong. He had to resist the love of the little boy up there on the bleachers, singing "Jingle Bell Rock" out of key with the rest of the kindergarteners. He had to resist the weakness. He was stronger than this.

His pager vibrated. He checked the number. Work. The cavalry had ridden in at the last moment, offering him the perfect defense. Whatever it was, he was glad for the excuse to push away from Sarah.

"It's my soldier in I.C.U." He spoke low as he grabbed his coat off the back of the chair. "I've got to go."

"I'll keep him in my prayers," she whispered, glancing up from her video recorder. "You'll call?"

"Promise." He could not turn away from her face, her dear face, radiant with love for him. Unmistakable love. His defenses were down, and Mike felt that hit full force. He reeled. A direct hit.

He turned without answering her, forcing his feet to carry him down the long, dark aisle and out the door to safety. He breathed in the cold night air, his breath rising in great misty clouds, and the children's voices followed him. The door swung closed, mercifully cutting off all ties of the woman and child tugging at him with impossible strength.

He kept going, jogging toward his truck. His footsteps echoed in the parking lot. There was a young soldier in I.C.U. who needed him, so he kept going, shutting off his heart, severing those ties pulling at him.

Sarah was right, he realized, taking out his keys. He *had* kept her at a distance. He was still doing it.

She had been right all along.

Sarah held back Ali's covers. "Okay, sweetie, climb in. Now it's time for a good night's sleep."

Ali, who had just finished his prayers, hopped to his feet and dove between the camouflage-printed sheets. "Sleep? I wanna stay up with you. I wanna watch the lights blink."

"They will still be blinking tomorrow. Now, lie down."

He dropped onto his pillow with a thump. "Mike didn't get to say goodbye. We gotta call him."

"He's probably in the operating room. We can't reach him there."

Ali snapped his fingers, all out of options. "I can't wait for the party."

"It will come faster if you close your eyes and go to sleep." She covered him up, snug as a bug and kissed his forehead. "You have sweet dreams, sweet boy."

"I love you, Sarah." Ali beamed up at her. "I love you like a mommy."

"I love you like my own little boy." Tears blurred her vision.

Now, please, God, let the adoption go through without a hitch. She gathered a shaky breath, hoped her knees would carry her out of the room and turned off the light switch with a trembling hand. It wasn't easy opening her heart even wider. It wasn't safe, but it was the right way to live. Even if she might lose him, she was going to love him with all her might.

And Mike, too.

"Good night, sweetie."

"'Night, Sarah."

Although the last few nights had been nightmare-free, she left the door open a crack to listen, just in case. The living room was quiet, the TV off and the Christmas tree lights blinking joyfully. Clarence lifted his head off the back of the couch as she passed by and offered a brief rusty purr. She stopped to rub his ears the way he liked it, and earned even more purring before he lowered his head, satisfied, and dismissed her.

Funny guy. She went to the entry closet and pulled out her wrapping paper storage container. She carried it to the table and popped it open. Chances were good that Ali wasn't asleep yet, so she would wrap his presents last.

"Don't look, Clarence," she told him as she pulled two sacks from the pet store out of the closet.

She carried the bags to the table and sorted through the many rolls of bright Christmas paper. Mike. She wondered how he was doing. She had already said prayers for his patient. If she didn't hear from him soon, she would say more.

She chose reindeer printed paper for the sack of catnip mice and laid the roll on the table. Tonight had been perfect. Ali's burdens were lighter. He sure seemed to have had fun. Dinner had been a blast, talking about the little things in their day and enjoying one another's company. The concert had been adorable. She had already watched the tape of it three times.

And there had been the kiss. The most perfect kiss ever. Gently sweet, it had filled her with dreams. Dreams that were coming true. Mike didn't have to say it for her to know that he loved her. She had felt it in his kiss and read it in his eyes. It had been in every look and warmed his every word.

She grabbed the scissors from the top compartment of the storage container and began to cut. Was that a squeak of Ali's bed frame? Was he up? She forgot her wrapping and tiptoed down the hall, going quietly in case she was wrong and listened for signs of his distress.

She heard little feet on the carpet and then silence. Not exactly what she was expecting. She crept down the hallway, straining to hear. Was he getting one of his stuffed animals, or was he having some sort of problem?

His nightlight made a soft glow in the corner, casting just enough light for her to see through the cracked door and into the room where Ali, in silhouette, knelt in prayer.

"God, can I please have a daddy? I got one all picked out. Mike's real nice. He plays ball real good."

Sarah stepped away, leaving Ali to his praying. So, she wasn't the only one who had felt it tonight. They had become a family, not officially, but one of the heart. It had happened quietly without any of them noticing, and now it was too late to deny it. She couldn't have a better Christmas gift.

And Mike? She hoped, how she prayed, that she and Ali were Mike's holiday wish.

The phone remained silent as she passed by it, and she thought about calling him. Just leaving him an encouraging voice mail. She knew how hard he worked. Maybe a text message. She would think on it some more.

"Clarence!" She stepped into the dining room and shook her head at the cat. He was on the table looking at her with a serene expression. He rolled onto his side and tossed a catnip mouse into the air. Christmas for him had come early, too.

The young soldier's wife was crying when he left her. The muffled sound of relief and fear followed him down the long shadowed corridor, echoing against the barren walls and in the lost places within him. The tiny place left of his soul hurt like it had been hit with artillery fire. He'd been able to give the young woman little hope and no comfort. The most that he could say was that her husband of thirteen months was still fighting.

It wasn't enough. He had fought with everything he had for the young man's life. For Zack, who was only nineteen. He had his whole life ahead of him, a nice wife and a kid on the way.

Weary, Mike rubbed his face. He was walking, his feet taking him down another long corridor. He felt restless, as if he could never be at peace again. He had blamed it on his deployment, on the stress and trauma and endless casualties, between the military and the civilians, and the inevitable death. The loss of life he couldn't hold back weighed on him until he couldn't breathe.

He ducked into the first doorway and stumbled to one of the back benches. Soft light from lit candles flickered like hope against the encroaching darkness. He buried his face in his hands and sat there, at rest but more tired than ever, paring down his feelings until he felt nothing, nothing at all. One day he was going to forget how. He was going to close down his heart late at night and come morning, it would be closed for good. It was coming sooner rather than later.

Maybe even now.

His phone buzzed. He'd turned it to vibrate after he'd seen Zack through recovery. He checked the screen before answering it. A text message from Sarah. It was 2:00 a.m. What was she still doing up?

He hit the Read button and her note popped up. *Just wanted to say hi. Know that I'm praying for you and your soldier. Hang in there.*

He closed his eyes and snapped his phone shut. He sat in silence for a long time, struggling to feel something. Fighting to feel anything. He thought of her tonight, with her delicate wholesomeness and beauty. He thought of how her laughter could warm him when nothing else could, like hot cocoa on a cold winter's morning. She was handing him what he needed most, her comfort, her encouragement, a soft place to land when he was falling hard and fast.

And it was too late. He'd already hit ground. He shoved the phone into his pocket. She was a dream he could not have. He had nothing left. Not for Sarah. Not for Ali. Not even for himself.

Chapter Fourteen

While her dear little students were making all kinds of noise squirming and fidgeting in their seats instead of coloring, Sarah hefted the box of gift bags from beneath her desk, where she had put them this morning for safekeeping.

It hadn't been the best morning. He had promised to call today. She had slept fitfully, wondering about Mike. She hadn't heard from him. How was his wounded soldier doing? She feared no news was bad news. It wasn't easy pasting a smile on her face, but she did so for her kids.

"Are y'all ready to get this party started?" she called out above their noise.

A chorus of affirmations rang out loud enough to hurt her eardrums. There was nothing like a holiday party on the last day before Christmas break to put kids in the best mood. Definitely something to celebrate. As long as she didn't think about Mike's silence, she didn't have to start worrying and doubting, and she could concentrate on celebrating, too.

"Merry Christmas, Ellie." Sarah put the first bag on Ellie Saunders's desk and the next one on Paige Paterson's desk. "Merry Christmas, Paige."

Ali was next. He was hard at work coloring away at what looked like a green triangle. "A Christmas tree."

"So I see." She set his gift bag on the edge of his desk and moved on. She could hear the students who had opened their bags exclaiming, and more expectant faces had turned toward her, their coloring forgotten.

Time to speed up the process. She heard a knock at her door. Could it be the surprise she had planned? She gave Josie Mayhew her bag and glanced over her shoulder. She could see them through the little window. There was a man and woman standing together hand in hand.

"Ellie, would you please go see who is at the door?" Sarah continued passing out gift bags, moving faster now that their guests of honor had arrived. "Y'all remember our adopted soldiers, right?"

Paige's hand shot in the air. "Miss Alpert? It's them. They're at the door."

"That's right. Whitney is well, and she and John are here, just as they promised they would be." That had been so long ago, it seemed. Before Mike's return and Ali came into her life.

Ellie held open the door and the guests of honor, whole and healed and joyful, walked into the room, their hands linked. Despite their hardships at war so far away from home, they looked calm and centered.

Maybe because they had their faith and one another to lean on, to share with and to love.

Sarah thought of Mike. He had been alone during his deployment. It hadn't been good for him. It wasn't the way God intended things to be. If only he would reach out to her.

She set a bag on the last child's desk. "John and Whitney, welcome. We're so happy to have you. You both look wonderful."

"We're glad to be here, Sarah." Whitney's smile beamed as she looked to her husband, the man who had remained unfailingly at her side. "Merry Christmas. Thank you everyone for your cards and letters. Your happy voices in those letters stayed with me even when I was sick and helped me to get better. I just want to give you all a great, big hug."

Chaos erupted. Little chairs squeaked against the floor and the thumping of a dozen pairs of feet herded Whitney's way. Sarah let the kids go, blinking at the tears in her eyes. It was a miracle to see the young soldier alive and well. It was proof positive of what prayer and love and God could do.

"Come color with me, Whitney!" "Come sit with me, Whitney." "John, look at this." "We're havin' cupcakes." The children's voices rang out with happiness, the most miraculous sound of all.

She took a moment to slip her cell out of her pocket and check the screen. Her ringer was silenced, but there had been no new calls or messages. Nothing from Mike. He could have worked all night and be sleeping today, or back at work. She shouldn't take it personally.

The thing was, she knew Mike. Was he regretting their kiss? Was he coming to the conclusion that they may have had a great time together last night, but that he still couldn't open his heart to her?

Worry about it later, Sarah. She tapped out a quick message. *I hope you are ok,* and hit Send. The kids were tugging Whitney and John over to the desks. It was time to bring out the cupcakes.

It had been another tough day and coming home just made things tougher. He closed the refrigerator door and there was the kid's picture. Maybe it was his sleep deprivation, but those memories had faded as if years instead of months had passed.

That didn't mean he didn't love the little fella. Mike popped the top of the can and took a long swig of iced tea. He let the cool tartness sweep down his throat, cooling him from the inside out. He turned his back on the picture, wishing he could find himself, wishing he knew what to do.

You're tired is all, he told himself. His defenses weren't as strong.

So why did he keep remembering kissing Sarah? He could try to convince himself it didn't mean anything, that it was only because of the mistletoe and the café owner's urging. But it was more than that. He had wanted to kiss her. He wanted to remember loving her.

Nothing. He felt nothing at all. He wasn't himself.

He didn't know who that was anymore. All he knew was that there was nothing left. Of him. Of his memories of her. Of their love. He felt like a man drowning, going down for the third time, praying to God he could miraculously swim.

He took another pull of tea and reached for his phone. Her message was there, caring as always. That was Sarah. He didn't deserve her. Not by a long shot.

I'm coming over after Ali is in bed. Meet me outside. He hit the Send button. He tried to picture Sarah in her cozy kitchen, probably doing dishes this time of night, with Ali chatting away and that cat of hers snoozing on the couch. Then would come TV time and story time. The Christmas lights would be flashing and there would be a mound of presents under the tree.

He had already done his Christmas shopping. It hadn't been hard. He had no family, not anymore. Ali's gifts were in a sack in the bedroom closet, along with a little something for Sarah. He knew she would love it. And there was one more thing he couldn't forget to give her. The photo album he had made for Ali.

It had taken all his spare time when he had been overseas to track down the photographs of Ali's family members who died. Mike felt nothing remembering the often dangerous trips with a few of his special forces buddies along for protection from insurgents to visit friends of Ali's mother. He felt nothing now at how kind the villagers had been, offering up sometimes their few remembrances for the little boy.

Mike's hand shook as he stared at the Message Sent screen. He was doing the right thing in making a clean break. He would apologize to her, give her the gifts and the album and stand strong on his own two feet. That's what he had to do. He didn't feel anything.

He wished that he could.

The anxiety gripping her stomach worsened when she saw Mike's shadow cross her lawn. She had been waiting for his truck to turn into her driveway. All evening long she had been unsettled not knowing. Was he regretting getting closer to her? Or did it have something to do with his own post-traumatic stress?

She clutched her coat around her and closed the door behind her. As Mike came closer, the glow of the Christmas twinklers flashed over him as if drawing him into the light, but he stood shadowed, as if in darkness. He looked grim.

Her knees went weak. She sank heavily to the top step. Had she let her hopes get too high? Had her only chance for happiness with him passed her by?

Bags rustled as he came closer. Shopping bags full of wrapped gifts. He towered over her, a stone pillar of darkness.

She longed for the buttery rich sound of his voice. She ached for the gentle lilt of his laughter.

He set the bags on the step in front of her. He seemed as if he were standing a thousand miles away from her. When he spoke, his voice sounded hollow. "Thought I would bring these over while I could. They have me working tomorrow and the next day. since I don't have any family."

He was working both holiday days? That didn't sound right. He had volunteered to work those days, that was her guess. Which meant he didn't want to be available to her and Ali. He didn't want to be with them. No—correct that—he didn't want to be with her.

He didn't love her.

Don't let him know how much that hurts, Sarah. She straightened her shoulders, struggling to sound as if she wasn't devastated. "I guess this means you won't be spending any part of Christmas with us."

"No, Sarah." Gentle those words.

It didn't lessen the pain. The first crack to her heart was like a hammer strike, and the second like a mallet. How could she let him go? Everything had been going so well. It was the kiss. It was too soon. She should have known Mike would pull away in response, but this? This wasn't withdrawing a step, it was retreating from the field.

"I was kind of hoping that we could—" She couldn't finish. Her eyes burned. Her throat ached.

"Me, too." He clenched his fists. It was his only movement. He stood straight and strong, unmovable. "I had hoped, but I was wrong."

The third crack to her heart was like a jackhammer. She loved this man, truly loved him, even when he was tearing her heart out. "I thought we were getting along really well."

"We were. I just can't do this. Not when we know how it will end."

Agony rolled over her like a riptide. "I wouldn't have made you choose this time."

"Sarah, that's not it. Please, I don't want you to cry."

"I'm not." She lifted her chin, blinking fast. Really, she wasn't crying. Her world was coming apart, but she wasn't going to break down. "How am I going to say goodbye to you? All the time that you were away, I kept hoping that we could try again. I wanted a second chance with you."

He hung his head, as if he didn't know how to answer. He didn't move, stoic and distant and in perfect self-control. "I'll always want the best for you, Sarah."

Goodbye. He was about to say it when she wanted to hold him close. When she needed his comfort and the shelter of his arms. Only his love could make this pain stop. "I'll always keep you in my prayers, Mike. Always."

As if she could ever stop hoping, ever stop loving this man who was her very own knight in shining armor. A heroic man who spent his life trying to save others. Who went beyond the call of duty. To whom courage and sacrifice was a daily act. She would always love him with a devotion that grew deeper by the hour, whether they were together or apart.

"Sarah, you're crying." He came to her side. Tenderly he cradled her face in his hands and brushed away her tears with the pads of his thumbs.

Tears streamed down her cheeks, unwanted and unstoppable. She would give anything to have the privilege of being with him. She thought of the future she'd began to dream of again gone—a small, storybook wedding, making supper with Mike when he was able to be home and instant messaging him when he wasn't. More children one day, both adopted and their own. They would build a life together, a family and a love so strong that it would make the world a better place.

Those dreams were gone now, vanished in the chilly air.

"It's not your fault, Sarah. It's mine." He looked lost in the shadows, a part of the darkness. His voice was layered with pain and defeat and self-anger.

She could feel his despair, worse than her own. "What do you mean? You are not completely at fault, Mike."

"I made the choice to walk away from you." His throat worked. "I regret how I treated you."

That made two of them. The final crack to her heart. It was over, and still she was looking for a way to hold on to hope. To hold on to Mike.

"You were right." He pulled away, leaving her tears to fall. "I *was* wrong. I did keep you at a distance. I blamed you for not loving me enough, when that's what I was doing. I was never going to let you get close to me. I'm just not made that way, Sarah. I'll never be what you need."

"Mike, we've both made mistakes." She sat still, watching him with pleading eyes. "Please, don't go. I don't want this to be over."

"It is." He had failed her. The one woman he loved more than he thought was possible. He would lay down his life for her in a second. He would move mountains for her. He would leave her now, because he was only going to cause her more pain. That was one thing his heart couldn't take more of.

His pager vibrated. His soldier in I.C.U. again. He didn't need to look to know that it was work. It was just the excuse he needed to find the courage to walk away from the best woman he had ever known.

"Goodbye, Sarah." He pushed to his feet. He had thought he could feel nothing anymore. He had thought there was nothing left within him.

But he'd been wrong. As he walked away from her, grief flattened him.

Chapter Fifteen

Sarah couldn't move. She didn't know if it was shock that kept her on the top step or sorrow. She was too numb to feel anything. Mortal wounds were like that, or so she had heard—too severe to deal with at first. But slowly the pain set in, dull and growing sharper until it was unbearable.

The cold wind gusted, blowing straight through her. The blink, blink of the lights were a rhythmic reminder of each passing second, one just like the rest, as the taillights of Mike's truck grew smaller down the street. He turned the corner and vanished, leaving behind the cheerful holiday displays of lights on the other houses.

The image of him standing before her and the flat note of his voice haunted her. She rubbed her eyes and realized she was crying. Not for herself, but for him.

His confession rattled around in her mind. *I blamed you for not loving me enough, when that's what I was doing. I was never going to let you get close to me.*

That wasn't right. It wasn't what he said, so much

as the way he'd said it. It was as if a cloud of deep despair clung to him like the night shadows. He spoke as if he had no heart left. As if he were a drowning man going down for the third time and no help in sight.

She swiped at her wet cheeks. The door behind her squeaked open a few inches. She had left it ajar and she smiled at Clarence who paced toward her, offering a meow of concern.

"Come here, handsome." She lifted him into her arms, savoring his silky softness and purring comfort. She climbed to her feet and carried him back into the house.

She lingered on the doorstep and took one long last look down the street, quiet and still this time of night, remembering the ghost of the man who had knelt before her, apologizing and brushing at her wet cheeks.

A month after Ali left we found ourselves under attack. She remembered standing in Mike's kitchen making spaghetti sauce and how he had gone stone cold when he mentioned the skirmish. His look of utter failure when he talked about the Army Ranger he had lost on his table.

Mike was a strong man, one of the mightiest she knew but maybe this kind of stress wasn't something even the strongest soldier ought to handle on his own. No man was an island; it wasn't a matter of strength. It was the way God had made us to love and need one another.

She felt devastated all over again. Mike was hurting, and he was suffering alone. Her heartbreak seemed small by comparison.

Clarence jumped out of her arms and onto his favored

spot on the back of the couch. He curled up and watched her with slitted eyes as she went back outside to fetch the gift bags. Mike. He had gone to a lot of trouble shopping and wrapping Ali's gifts *early* instead of his usual last minute. That said everything right there. He loved the little boy more than he wanted to admit.

She locked the door against the cold and night. Why had he given up trying to adopt Ali? He had said at the time that he had the army. If he believed that, he never would have wanted to adopt a child in the first place. No, this was about something larger, she realized, something that Mike had kept to himself, as he did most things.

She set the bags down by the tree and began to unload them. Wouldn't Ali be surprised in the morning? That would be a great way to start Christmas Eve day, since the boy would miss seeing his hero over the holidays.

She carefully set one present after another beneath the cheerful tree. She had been overwhelmed with her own disappointment, shattered dreams for true love could do that to a girl, and then worried over Mike, she hadn't gotten to the real issue. Ali was going to be devastated.

How did this turn into such a big mess, Lord? How am I going to save this little boy from more loss? Maybe I should have protected him more, but that would have meant not seeing Mike. They need each other.

I need them, too. That was the truth, straight from her soul. Her life was better with Mike and Ali in it.

Brighter. More meaningful. Beyond that, they were her purpose. She was meant to love them.

Show me what to do, Lord. I can't see it through all my heartbreak. Please, Father, send me a sign. Something. I am lost here.

She felt no answer but when she ended her prayer and opened her eyes she felt stronger, as if she were no longer alone. She pulled the last gift out of the bottom of the first bag. It was small, not tiny, but just the right size for a boxed ornament. She smiled. Mike used to get her one of her favorite porcelain collectable ornaments every year to hang on her tree. Maybe he had found a little soldier ornament for Ali.

She set the gift on the pile beneath the tree, and the purple glow of a single lightbulb reflected off the red ribbon, catching her attention. The tag had her name on it. It was a gift for her.

Sarah, I thought this would be a reminder of your first Christmas with Ali, Mike had written.

She opened it without thinking, trembling and breathless. She hadn't expected this. Once the paper was off, she pried the lid up. The truth hit her when she saw the dear figurine of a dark-haired little boy holding a string of Christmas lights.

The hour was late and the hospital chapel was the closest thing to peace he could find. Not that he wanted to admit it. Mike rested his forehead in his hands, so sick at heart he didn't know how to cope anymore.

Footsteps warned him of someone approaching. He

straightened up on the bench and tried to pull it together. The last thing he wanted was for anyone to see him like this.

"Mike." Franklin Fields padded into the chapel. "I came by to see your young soldier and his wife. Congratulations. He's out of I.C.U."

Mike forced a smile. He respected Franklin. "Zach got lucky. He was able to pull through."

"It wasn't luck, Mike." Franklin took the end of the bench. "You're a talented surgeon. According to those in the know, one of the best they've seen."

"It's not me." He hated the helplessness of it. The failure of watching one patient die and another live under the same circumstances, with the same prognosis. Of helping one to fight to live while another less wounded died. He hung his head. "I wish it was me, but it isn't."

"Let me guess. You got into medicine because you wanted to help save people. Because you value life."

He nodded. "Plus there was the benefit of long hours and army pay."

That lightened the mood, but not much. Franklin's smile was brief. "It's God working through you, Mike. The way He works good through everyone, even those who think relying on Him is a weakness."

"I don't want to be converted, Franklin. No offense."

"That's not what I'm saying, Mike." The pastor had a quiet authority that was hard not to respect. "You are here for a reason, and it isn't because you wanted a quiet room. There are plenty of places here that are quiet this time of night. And I can't convert you. The answers are for you to find. I can only sit with you while you do."

"Then you're wasting your time, reverend."

"It's my time to waste." Franklin shrugged. "Anything else you want to talk about? I know you had a tough deployment."

"How do you know that?"

"I've counseled other soldiers you served with, for one. But all I need to do is look at you. You look troubled, son, as if you have a world of burden on your soul."

"Some days it feels that way." Mike wished—he even prayed—that he could feel something, anything, that would bring him back to life.

"Christ sacrificed His life so that others could live. He lived His life in service to others."

"Thanks, but I can do this my way. Standing on my own two feet. No offense, Franklin."

"None taken. I know how it is. It's tough to open up. It's the way you learn to cope keeping your wounds to yourself. I used to feel it was weak to open up. Then I realized it was wrong to shy away from living life. Sometimes you have to take a leap of faith in God and in love."

Sarah. Mike squeezed his eyes shut but still the image came to him of her sitting on her front steps, gilded with the jeweled shine of the Christmas decorations with tears on her cheeks. He had hurt her, but how could he be with her? He was dying inside. He couldn't expose her to that.

"Are you all right?" Franklin asked.

He managed a single nod and opened his eyes. Candles sputtered on the altar, and that's how he was inside.

"You are one of the strongest men I know, Mike. Take some advice. Sometimes God hands you a lifeline. You've got to be strong enough to take it."

"Sarah."

"Yes." Franklin pushed his card across the bench and stood. "And that little boy who needs you. Maybe it is His way of letting you know you aren't alone. When you are lost, don't despair. That's when you find what matters most."

Mike pressed his hands to his face, praying he had enough strength left.

Chapter Sixteen

Bleary-eyed, Mike drove toward home. Dawn was coming, although it was hard to tell because of the clouds. It had been a long night, but at least he knew what he had to do. He had fallen asleep in the night room. He had just enough time to shower, change, grab a bite and head back. With any luck, he would have enough time to stop by Sarah's house on the way into work. He had a lot to say to her, things that could not be said over the phone.

He turned down his street, one house after another bright with Christmas lights. It was Christmas Eve. For the first time he could feel the hope of the season in his heart. He slowed down as he neared his driveway. What was going on?

Multicolored lights flashed along the rail of his small porch. It looked like there was a wreath on his front door, and Sarah's SUV parked in his driveway.

It was his answered prayer to see Sarah step out from

behind her SUV, graced by the soft glow of lights. He pulled to a stop, catching the culprits in his headlights. There was a box of ornaments in her arms and a tree leaning against the back of her vehicle.

Sarah, his beautiful, gentle Sarah. For the first time his heart sparked like a candle, newly lit. He wanted to feel more. He needed to feel more. He cut the engine and stepped out into the bitterly cold morning.

"Mike!" Ali came racing out from behind Sarah, bundled in his warm winter coat and hat with the ball on top. "Look at the lights."

"I see. Those are pretty fine lights."

"Yep. You know what?"

"What?"

"You gotta have lights and a tree!" Ali wrapped his arms around Mike's waist and gave him a hug. "I'm bringin' you Christmas."

"Thanks, buddy. That's a mighty fine gift." There was such goodness in the world, too. He could see it now, even through his darker experiences. He needed this child with all of his heart. He returned Ali's hug and straightened, feeling better. Much better.

Now for Sarah. He steeled his self-control, this time to keep the guards on his heart down.

She was bundled up, too. Her cheeks and nose were pink from the cold and her eyes asked a question his heart could hear. "Any chance the invitation for Christmas still stands?"

"Pretty good."

"How good?"

"One hundred percent." She smiled, and it was like taking his first breath.

A little scary, but he needed her. He couldn't make it without her. He knew that now. "I can't believe you're here."

"Ali wanted to bring you Christmas, and I thought it was a very good idea. You need Christmas, and we need you."

"I pushed you away. I hurt you." He swallowed hard, digging deep for words that didn't come. There was no way around it. It shamed him. It also gave him hope. He had found what he had lost, what mattered most: the little boy standing at his side and the woman who was his everything. "I was going to come to you, but you beat me to it."

"I'm always going to be here for you, Mike."

Her understanding meant everything. He held out his hand and she came into his arms. He held her tightly with all the need in his soul, savoring the warmth of her in his arms. The lost pieces in him ached, found after all. Keeping his heart wide open, he went down to his knees in gratitude.

"Mike? Are you all right?" Concern lined her face. Love shone in her eyes.

"I'm fine. Never been better." He took her hand in his. He heard Ali gasp; the boy had figured out what Sarah had not yet realized. "I promised myself in the chapel—"

"You were in the chapel?" she interrupted, a little shocked.

"Yes." He wasn't going to be sidetracked. That discussion was for another time. This one could not wait. "I promised myself that the moment I saw you I was going to ask you a very important question."

"A question? Oh, Mike, you are down on your knees." Realization made her gasp. Tears sparkled like silver in her eyes. The frigid wind chose that moment to gust, dancing through her silken red hair. Her lower lip trembled. Never had she looked more lovely to him than with her whole heart revealed and vulnerable.

He took her hand, feeling the emotion tremble through her. He had put up defensive perimeters for as long as he could remember. But no more.

It was tough to let down his guard, tougher still to say what he had felt all this time, to say what had always been his truth. "You are my dream, Sarah. Come rain or shine, rough or still waters, I want to be right beside you, taking care of you, loving you, needing you."

"You need me?"

"More than air to breathe. More than the army. More than being a doctor. You are what I need to make my world right." He cleared his throat, taking time as the wind gusted harder and fine drizzle began to mist from the heavy sky. "You are my once-in-a-lifetime love, Sarah. I love you. Marry me, please, because I am lost without you."

"Yes. I will marry you." It was her Christmas wish come true. There was more than forgiveness; there was hope for a blissful future. Mike gazed up at her with love, and they both might be a little battered for what they had been through, but stronger, too. Sarah blinked, hoping her vision would clear, hoping she could find the right words. "I've never stopped loving you, Mike. I love you for exactly who you are. Everything you are."

"That's how I love you." He stood, towering over her, blocking her from the wind and rain. "Except there's one thing. I'm not going to go for another long engagement. If you want to be my wife, you will have to marry me right away."

"Funny, I feel the same exact way." Joy warmed her through, so that she didn't notice the inclement weather or the fact that the street was coming to life. A jogger trotted by. A neighbor across the street took his dog for a walk. "How does a January wedding sound to you?"

"Just right." His hands cradled her face. His touch was reverent, his tenderness unmistakable. "Thank you, Sarah. For bringing me Christmas. For being here. For not giving up on me."

"I made that mistake once, and I will never do it again." They had wasted so much time between the two of them with their mistakes and fears. But no more. Life was too precious and their love was too important. The army, having a family around his deployments, it was all things that they could work out. All she wanted was Mike to have and to hold forever as her husband, her love, her life. "Real love isn't letting go. It's holding on in rough waters."

"Then I'm going to hold on to you, Sarah, no matter what. You can count on that."

"We're two of a kind, Mike." Soul mates. Best friends. Forever in love. They had found their way back to one another. Love, real and true, bound them more tightly than any force in the universe. "I can't wait for our life to start. I have been waiting for so long."

"Me, too." He kissed her gently, as if he wanted her to feel all that was in his heart.

Sarah's soul sighed with contentment. She was right where she belonged at last. "There is only one problem. I'm not going to adopt Ali."

"What?" Mike stepped back, shocked by her words, searching her face before he smiled. "I agree. I think that your adopting Ali is a very bad decision."

"That's right. *We* are going to adopt him. Together."

"Together," Mike agreed with one hundred percent happiness. It shimmered in his beautiful hazel eyes and danced in the air between them.

"It's all white!" Ali jumped up, trying to catch as many snowflakes as he could in both hands. "Look, Mike! Look, Sarah!"

Tiny airborne flakes dusted the air. Snow, she realized in amazement. Tiny flakes sifted over them like Heavenly grace. It was the perfect start to their happy ending.

Epilogue

New Year's Eve

"Sarah, I can't believe this turnout for our fund-raiser." Caitlyn Villard sidled up in line at the refreshment counter. She radiated happiness that was brighter than the engagement ring she wore. Caitlyn gestured to the rink and the recreation area pleasantly congested with families. "It's our best yet."

"Think of all the world's children who will benefit." Sarah accepted her change from the cashier and pocketed it. There was so much need, but making a difference mattered. "How was your first Christmas with Amanda and Josie?"

"Mom, Steve and I did everything we could to make it a good one, but the girls are going to need time to adjust. That's why we are having a long engagement. The children come first."

"Yes they do." Sarah admired the love and care Caitlyn gave her sweet twin nieces. "Are they out on the ice?"

"Yes. Mom is keeping an eye on them." Caitlyn smiled as her fiancé came up behind her and put his hands on her shoulders. There was love in her eyes and in his.

There was nothing in this world more important than love. Sarah took the cardboard carrier of snow cones from the clerk and told Caitlyn and Steve she would see them on the ice.

"Sarah!" Anna Terenkov waved. She was hand in hand with her tall, dark handsome helicopter pilot David Ryland, who had flown Ali from the Middle East to the States.

They were clearly an item as they stood close together, looking deeply contented. Word was that David was going to finish out at Fort Bonnell and then work for the hospital as a medical helicopter pilot. The happy couple were talking with her mom. A very happy looking Olga waved, too, standing next to a transformed Reverend Franklin Fields, who nodded hello.

There were so many happy endings lately. Good people who deserved great happiness. She was deeply grateful to God for leading her back to Mike. Joy filled her as she spotted him out on the ice. Her heart skipped two beats at the sight of him strong and protective, skating alongside Ali. Their son. The paperwork was moving forward. The adoption would be complete soon, according to their attorney, Jake, who was supposed to be here along with his fiancée, Maddie.

She searched the crowd and saw them at the silent auction tables. Jake and Maddie looked like a perfect match in their Texas Longhorns sweatshirts and jeans, and the sight warmed her heart. Maddie, an army nurse, often visited Ali when he was in the hospital and was very fond of him. As was Jake, who was finalizing his adoption and setting up the college trust Ali's grandfather, Marlon, had left him, the dear old man. It was hard to miss the knockout marquis-cut diamond engagement ring on Maddie's left hand. She had heard from Jake that the couple were hoping to get married as soon as things could be arranged.

"Sarah, I've been looking for you." Robert Dale, reporter for the Midwest bureau of the *Liberty & Justice* headed her way with his arm around Dr. Nora Blake, who had been Ali's heart surgeon. Rob was a born charmer with his wavy brown hair, bright blue eyes and ready smile. "We saw Mike and Ali out on the ice."

"I love to see my patients happy and well." Nora smiled, and the intense, blond beauty had never looked happier. "I'm thankful his story has a good end."

"I am, too," Sarah agreed, thinking of all the needy children in the world, praying that they would find one, too. "So, what is the word on the two of you?"

"Now that I'm here at Fort Bonnell to stay," Rob said, "my next mission is to marry Nora."

"You are never going to get an easier assignment." Nora smiled.

After saying goodbye, Sarah headed down the aisle through the bleachers. She searched the ice. There they were: her boys. Love uplifted her. Ali proudly took short gliding steps while Mike cheered him on. Mike looked up and the moment their gazes met, their souls did, too.

She held up the box of cones, earning another smile. There were two blueberry ones for the boys, and a strawberry one for her. She carried them to an empty bench, and recognized two of the little girls from her class. Julia Saunders and Evan Paterson knelt before each of their children, busily lacing up their skates. Julia was Ali's social worker.

One of the best things about this fund-raiser was the chance it gave her to catch up with the people she cared about. She smiled at her students. "I'm glad you could make it tonight."

"Hi, Miss Alpert," Ellie and Paige said in unison.

"We wouldn't miss it for anything." Julia finished the bow on her daughter's skate and straightened. Anyone could see how happy finding Evan had made her. Her new engagement ring sparkled tastefully on her slender hand.

"Congratulations." Sarah leaned to admire the diamond. "When is the wedding?"

"Soon!" Julia radiated the kind of joy that only came from finding true love. The man at her side gazed at her the same way. "Sarah, I'm so pleased everything worked out with you and Mike. Now Ali has a family. He is loved."

"God is gracious." Sarah had never seen it so clearly before.

"Yes He is. Looks like your boys are here. We had best get out on the ice. We'll see you at Mike's baptism on Sunday." She and Evan took hands and the four of them went off together, their own happy little family.

Yes, God was very gracious. Her own hero dropped onto the bench beside her, guiding their little boy to make sure he didn't trip on his blades.

"Sarah? You know what?" Ali, bubbling with joy, dug into his snow cone. "I went around the rink all by myself! I didn't fall or anything."

Mike was silently laughing. She knew that look. He had made sure Ali had skated in victory, gently keeping a hand on him whenever he looked ready to fall.

She loved him greatly. It was so easy to see their future. Their wedding in three weeks, and their honeymoon—they were taking Ali to the theme parks in Florida. Mike might deploy late next year or maybe not. They didn't know for sure, but they were not going to put off having a baby and adopting another child. Heaven knew there was a world of need. She was proud to be marrying one of the soldiers who put service above self to fight for what mattered most.

"Are you doing anything after you're finished with your snow cone?" Mike leaned close to whisper in her ear.

"What did you have in mind?"

"A spin around the ice with my favorite girl." His smile became a kiss. "Happy New Year, Sarah. This is going to be our best year yet."

"I know it is. Our best is yet to come." She kissed

him back. Life was good, and she was incredibly lucky. Filled with love and brimming with hope, she thanked the Lord for all her beautiful blessings.

* * * * *

Dear Reader,

Thank you so much for choosing Homefront Holiday. I hope you enjoyed reading Sarah's story as much as I did writing it. Sarah regrets breaking off her relationship with Mike. Mike is a dedicated soldier and surgeon suffering from post-traumatic stress and life without Sarah. The little orphan Ali finds a new loving family with Sarah and Mike. I am very grateful to Steeple Hill books for allowing me to tell this story of deserving people who work toward forgiveness, love and healing. I love that this is a story where the good guys finish first. I hope you do, too.

Please drop by my Web site at www.jillianhart.net.

Blessings and Merry Christmas.

Jillian Hart

QUESTIONS FOR DISCUSSION

1. At the beginning of the story, how would you describe Sarah? What are her weaknesses and her strengths?

2. When Mike sees Sarah on the street for the first time since their breakup, how does he treat her? What does he believe? What does this say about his character?

3. How do Sarah's feelings for Mike change? Why?

4. Sarah is new to faith. She is learning to turn to the Lord. How is this evident?

5. Mike is struggling with the aftereffects of a difficult tour of duty. How does he cope? What does this say about him?

6. How is God's leading evident in the story?

7. How does Sarah forgive Mike? Why does she begin to see the importance of Mike's values and ideas?

8. Mike has worked hard and made great sacrifices for his country. Why has he done this? Why does he believe it is important?

9. How does Sarah come to understand Mike's great sense of duty? How does this change her?

10. Mike's view of faith softens throughout the story. What has kept him from accepting Christ into his heart? What finally breaks down his reserve?

11. How does Mike come to forgive Sarah?

12. How do the themes and values of Christmas work in this story?

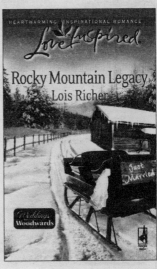

REQUEST YOUR FREE BOOKS!

2 FREE INSPIRATIONAL NOVELS
PLUS 2
FREE
MYSTERY GIFTS

LoveInspired.

YES! Please send me 2 FREE Love Inspired® novels and my 2 FREE mystery gifts (gifts are worth about $10). After receiving them, if I don't wish to receive any more books, I can return the shipping statement marked "cancel". If I don't cancel, I will receive 4 brand-new novels every month and be billed just $4.24 per book in the U.S. or $4.74 per book in Canada, plus 25¢ shipping and handling per book and applicable taxes, if any*. That's a savings of over 20% off the cover price! I understand that accepting the 2 free books and gifts places me under no obligation to buy anything. I can always return a shipment and cancel at any time. Even if I never buy another book, the two free books and gifts are mine to keep forever.

113 IDN ERXA   313 IDN ERWX

Name	(PLEASE PRINT)

Address	Apt. #

City	State/Prov.	Zip/Postal Code

Signature (if under 18, a parent or guardian must sign)

Order online at www.LoveInspiredBooks.com

Or mail to Steeple Hill Reader Service:

IN U.S.A.: P.O. Box 1867, Buffalo, NY 14240-1867
IN CANADA: P.O. Box 609, Fort Erie, Ontario L2A 5X3

Not valid to current subscribers of Love Inspired books.

Want to try two free books from another series?
Call 1-800-873-8635 or visit www.morefreebooks.com

* Terms and prices subject to change without notice. N.Y. residents add applicable sales tax. Canadian residents will be charged applicable provincial taxes and GST. Offer not valid in Quebec. This offer is limited to one order per household. All orders subject to approval. Credit or debit balances in a customer's account(s) may be offset by any other outstanding balance owed by or to the customer. Please allow 4 to 6 weeks for delivery. Offer available while quantities last.

Your Privacy: Steeple Hill Books is committed to protecting your privacy. Our Privacy Policy is available online at www.SteepleHill.com or upon request from the Reader Service. From time to time we make our lists of customers available to reputable third parties who may have a product or service of interest to you. If you would prefer we not share your name and address, please check here. ☐

LIREG08R

TITLES AVAILABLE NEXT MONTH

Don't miss these four stories in January

ROCKY MOUNTAIN LEGACY by Lois Richer
Weddings by Woodwards
A bride should have a say in the most important day of her life,
right? Not when her brother is Cade Porter. Star wedding planner
Sara Woodward thinks Cade is too arrogant when he takes over
his sister's wedding...until Cade assures Sara that when it comes
to *their* wedding she's in control.

A FAMILY FOR LUKE by Carolyne Aarsen
A family is not something Luke Harris has ever had, and it's
the only thing he wants. Yet his neighbor, overworked widow
Janie Corbett, is sure this helpful man is too good to be true.
With the help of Janie's three smart kids and one golden
Labrador, they both may find that love lives right next door.

MOMMY'S HOMETOWN HERO by Merrillee Whren
The woman he's loved since childhood has finally returned to
their small South Dakota town, and ex-soldier Matt Dalton is not
giving her up without a fight. Single mom Rachel Charbonneau
plans on leaving as soon as her family's farm is sold. Until Matt's
love and faith make him her hometown hero.

DADDY FOR KEEPS by Pamela Tracy
One look in those green eyes and bull rider Lucas "Lucky" Welch
knows the little boy in front of him is his late brother's son.
Things get even more complicated as he learns the truth behind
Robby's birth. Yet Lucky knows that if he hangs on tight he'll
show Natalie Crosby that he can be not just a daddy but a
husband for keeps.

LICNM1208BPA